*"I'm not alone. Logic is with me."*

SIGIZMUND KRZHIZHANOVSKY

# GLAS NEW RUSSIAN WRITING

## contemporary Russian literature

## in English translation

Volume 39

# Sigizmund Krzhizhanovsky

# Seven Stories

### Translated by Joanne Turnbull

glas

GLAS Publishers
tel./fax: +7(095)441-9157
perova@glas.msk.su
**www.russianpress.com/glas**

**Glas is distributed in North America by**
NORTHWESTERN UNIVERSITY PRESS
Chicago Distribution Center,
tel: 1-800-621-2736 or (773) 702-7000
fax: 1-800-621-8476 or (773)-702-7212
pubnet@202-5280
www.nupress.northwestern.edu

**in the UK and Europe by**
INPRESS LIMITED
Tel:  020 8832 7464
Fax:  020 8832 7465
stephanie@inpressbooks.co.uk
www.inpressbooks.co.uk

Editors: Natasha Perova & Joanne Turnbull
Front and back cover photographs by Moisei Nappelbaum (c. 1925)
Design by Tatiana Shaposhnikova

ISBN 5-7172-0073-0

# CONTENTS

Introduction
6

Map of the Arbat
12

Quadraturin
14

In the Pupil
29

The Runaway Fingers
70

Autobiography of a Corpse
81

The Unbitten Elbow
121

The Bookmark
136

Yellow Coal
184

Notes
203

# Introduction

Like a character in one of his stories, Sigizmund Krzhizhanovsky (1887-1950) has returned from oblivion. A prominent figure in literary circles first in Kiev then in Moscow in the 1920s and '30s, he was all but unpublished and, as he put it, "known for being unknown". The author of five short novels, more than a hundred stories, a dozen plays, screenplays and librettos, and dozens of essays, he worked in almost total obscurity.

The day Krzhizhanovsky died, Georgy Shengeli, the poet and critic, mourned the passing of "a writer-visionary, an unsung genius." If not for those words, discovered decades later by the scholar Vadim Perelmuter in Shengeli's diary, Krzhizhanovsky's oeuvre might have remained unmined in the archives in perpetuity.

Who was Krzhizhanovsky? No one knew. But Shengeli was known to have been very caustic towards his contemporaries. And the phrase "an unsung genius" came from a poem by Severyanin in praise of Leskov, another great writer neglected during his lifetime. The ensuing search for Krzhizhanovsky brought to light an otherworldly man of enormous erudition (a student of astronomy, mathematics, literature, philosophy, languages — he knew ten) who was constitutionally incapable of accommodating the coarse commissars of Soviet culture. His terse, metaphorical, clearly modernist prose was marked by hyperbole, irony, paradox and phantasms. "A fantastical plot is my method," he wrote.

"First you borrow from reality, you ask reality for permission to use your imagination, to deviate from actual fact; later you repay your debt to your creditor with nature, with a profoundly realistic investigation of the facts and an exact logic of conclusions."

Not until 1989 could Krzhizhanovsky's subtly subversive writings begin to be published. Only now are his collected works — some 3,000 pages — being brought out in Russian. Critics today compare him to Kafka and Borges, Swift and Gogol. To that list one might also add Beckett.

Born in Kiev to a Polish Catholic family, Krzhizhanovsky was the youngest of five children, the only son, very musical. He might have become a professional musician but instead took two degrees at Kiev University — in law and in classical philology. The Bolshevik Revolution put an end to his career as a lawyer, freeing him to devote all of his time to writing and philosophy. Two earlier summers spent abroad — in Switzerland, France, Italy and Germany — now inspired a pair of essays. Then in 1919, Krzhizhanovsky published what he would later call his first *real* story: "Якоби и 'Якобы'" — a "fantasy-dialogue" between Jacobi, the German philosopher, and "Supposedly", the sum of all human meanings.

At the same time, Krzhizhanovsky was becoming popular in Kiev as a lecturer — on the psychology of creativity, on the history and theory of the theater, on literature and music. In 1920, he began collaborating with Anna Bovshek, the former Moscow Art Theater actress who would become his lifelong companion. They devoted their first joint performance to Adalbert von Chamisso, the German poet and botanist, and his "Strange Story of Peter Schlemihl" — about an impecunious young man who gives up his shadow to the devil in exchange for an inexhaustible purse.

In the spring of 1922 Bovshek left Kiev for Moscow, soon to be followed by Krzhizhanovsky. Friends had given him several letters of introduction to Muscovites who might help him to find a room. One letter, to Nikolai Berdyaev, the religious philosopher, led nowhere; but another letter, to Ludmila Severtsova, wife of the evolutionist, produced lodgings at Number 44 on the Arbat. Apartment 5 was the home of an elderly count. The count invited Krzhizhanovsky (very tall, thin, slightly stooped, with a pale nervous face and wearing a pince-nez) to inhabit a small, dark room at the end of the corridor. Six square meters (65 square feet), unfurnished. The writer added a wooden bed with a horsehair mattress, a table with two drawers, an armchair with a hard seat, and hanging bookshelves. Rather than take money for the room, the count suggested that Krzhizhanovsky take paid English lessons from him. The lessons were short-lived: the count soon died, the countess moved out, and less sympathetic neighbors moved in to what would become that hallmark of Soviet life, a communal apartment.

It was in that viewless "quadrature" — so small it must once have been a maid's room or perhaps a larder — that Krzhizhanovsky wrote his philosophical, satirical, lyrical phantasmagorias. It was in that room that he wrote six of the seven remarkable stories in this collection.

Three of the seven — "Quadraturin", "Autobiography of a Corpse" and "The Book Mark" — belong to a cycle of stories called *What Men Die By*. This title recalls "What Men Live By", a parable by Tolstoy in which an angel is sent down to earth to discover what men live by. He finds that men live (and thrive) not by caring for themselves, but by loving each other: "He who loves is in God and God is in him, for God is love." In *What Men Die By*, God is dead: the heroes are intent on looking after themselves and what they think is their own best interest.

Krzhizhanovsky called himself a satirist (in the Swiftian sense) and an experimental realist. The Soviet literary establishment had little use for either. The surreal horror and black humor of a story like "Quadraturin" (about the trials of a man who is given a substance which expands his cramped living quarters ad infinitum) was at odds with official injunctions to portray the "revolutionary reality" in a positive light.

Two of the stories included here — "The Runaway Fingers" and "The Unbitten Elbow" — were printed. But they are exceptions. The editors to whom Krzhizhanovsky brought his fictions mostly handed them back: they were "not timely", they said, "not contemporary".

Life in hungry, unheated Moscow during the dislocated 1920s was hand-to-mouth for many, let alone an impecunious and ideologically suspect writer from Kiev. Mikhail Bulgakov termed his own struggle for a foothold in the capital "the blackest period of my life": "My wife and I are starving," he noted in his diary. "I've run all over Moscow — there's no work. My felt boots have fallen apart." Kzhizhanovsky, too, would soon be dogged by "Doctor Shrott" — his euphemism for hunger. (In Germany there was a sanatorium by that doctor's name, which treated hunger victims.) "Doctor Shrott follows me about, but I deftly manage to avoid face-to-face encounters," he wrote to Bovshek in Odessa. "I do wish that old man would give me the slip, or maybe lose my address."

In 1932, a friend of a friend approached Maksim Gorky with, among other things, "In the Pupil". An advocate of Socialist Realism, Gorky dismissed Krzhizhanovsky's stories as old-fashioned and irrelevant: "Most of mankind has no time for philosophy." (Fifty years later a Moscow editor would reject them again — because Gorky had rejected them in the first place.)

"A thinker," said Krzhizhanovsky, "is not someone who thinks loyally, but someone who is loyal to his thoughts." He did his thinking sitting on boulevard benches, striding about the streets of Moscow, lying on the couch at Anna Bovshek's. What mattered most to him, she later wrote, was the logic of his conclusions. Many of his stories have the quality of a problem or puzzle: "I am interested," he said, "not in the arithmetic, but in the algebra of life."

Even before Gorky's expressed displeasure, Bovshek had feared for her non-conformist friend: "In the morning I never knew how the night had gone, or if he had woken up in his own bed." The two continued to live apart and to meet in the evenings. Though Krzhizhanovsky's room was small, even by Soviet standards, his neighbors hated him: they found his habits odd, his behavior suspicious, and sometimes a woman would spend the night. Bovshek entreated him to come and live with her in her larger, more comfortable room at 3 Zemledelchesky Lane, but he insisted he needed a room of his own. He also felt, she later recalled, that life in one apartment would destroy the enchantment of their relationship. ("In the Pupil" is in part a reflection of their unusual arrangement.) Krzhizhanovsky's manuscripts, however, did live at Bovshek's — hidden in her wardrobe under a shroud-like length of gold-embroidered black brocade. She worried about them too.

One collection of stories had been accepted in 1924 by a cooperative publishing house, which then folded. In 1928 another collection was being typeset when the censors ordered the composition undone. A third collection met the same fate six years later. In 1941 a final collection (including the anti-utopia "Yellow Coal") made its way past the censors only to be stopped by the German invasion.

With that, Krzhizhanovsky stopped writing stories. He made translations, he gave lectures, and — like the hero of "The Bookmark" — gave away the "themes" with which his imagination continued to fountain in casual conversation. Alcohol became an indispensable crutch. Asked what had brought him to wine, he joked: "A sober attitude towards reality." Dangerously ill, he finally moved in with Bovshek at the end of 1949. The neighbors ranted about this "illegal" resident (he and Bovshek had never married). A stroke soon deprived him of the ability to read. He tried unsuccessfully to relearn the alphabet. On 28 December 1950, Shengeli drew a black frame around this entry in his diary: "Today Sigizmund Dominikovich Krzhizhanovsky died, a writer-visionary, an unsung genius."

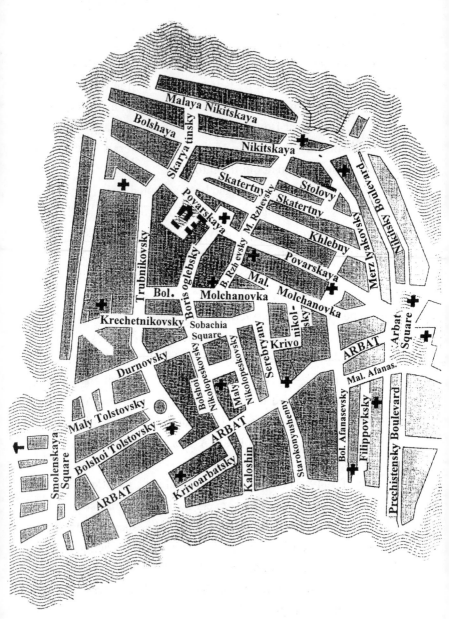

The Arbat, neighboring streets and churches in the 1920s

# Sigizmund Krzhizhanovsky

## Seven Stories

# Quadraturin

## 1

From outside there came a soft knock at the door: once. Pause. And again — a bit louder and bonier: twice.

Sutulin, without rising from his bed, extended — as was his wont — a foot towards the knock, threaded a toe through the door handle, and pulled. The door swung open. On the threshold, head grazing the lintel, stood a tall, grey man the colour of the dusk seeping in at the window.

Before Sutulin could set his feet on the floor the visitor stepped inside, wedged the door quietly back into its frame and, jabbing first one wall, then another, with a briefcase dangling from an apishly long arm, said, "Yes: a matchbox."

"What?"

"Your room, I say: it's a matchbox. How many square feet?"

"Eighty-six and a bit."

"Precisely. May I?"

And before Sutulin could open his mouth, the visitor sat down on the edge of the bed and hurriedly unbuckled his bulging briefcase. Lowering his voice almost to a whisper, he went on, "I'm here on business. You see, I, that is, we, are conducting, how shall I put it... well, experiments, I suppose. Under wraps for now. I won't hide the fact: a well-known foreign firm has an interest in our concern. You want the electric-light switch? No, don't bother: I'll only be a minute. So then: we have discovered — this is a secret now — an agent for biggerizing rooms. Well, won't you try it?"

The stranger's hand popped out of the briefcase and proffered Sutulin a narrow dark tube, not unlike a tube of paint, with a tightly screwed cap and a leaden seal. Sutulin fidgeted bewilderedly with the slippery tube and, though it was nearly dark in the room, made out on the label the clearly printed word: **Quadraturin**. When he raised his eyes, they came up against the fixed, unblinking stare of his interlocutor.

"So then, you'll take it? The price? Goodness, it's gratis. Just for advertising. Now if you'll" — the guest began quickly leafing through a sort of ledger he had produced from the same briefcase — "just sign this book (a short testimonial, so to say). A pencil? Have mine. Where? Here: column III. That's it."

His ledger clapped shut, the guest straightened up, wheeled round, stepped to the door... and a minute later Sutulin, having snapped on the light, was considering with puzzledly raised eyebrows the clearly embossed letters: **Quadraturin**.

On closer inspection it turned out that this zinc packet was tightly fitted — as is often done by the makers of patented agents — with a thin transparent paper whose ends were expertly glued together. Sutulin removed the paper sheath from the Quadraturin, unfurled the rolled-up text, which showed through the paper's transparent gloss, and read:

DIRECTIONS

Dissolve 1 teaspoon of the Quadraturin essence in 1 cup of water. Wet a piece of cotton wool or simply a clean rag with the solution; apply this to those of the room's internal walls designated for proliferspansion. This mixture leaves no stains, will not damage wallpaper, and even contributes — incidentally — to the extermination of bedbugs.

Thus far Sutulin had been only puzzled. Now his puzzlement was gradually overtaken by another feeling, strong and disturbing. He stood up and tried to pace from corner to corner, but the corners of this living cage were too close together: a walk amounted to almost nothing but turns, from toe to heel and back again. Sutulin stopped short, sat down and, closing his eyes, gave himself up to thoughts, which began: Why not...? What if...? Suppose...? To his left, not three feet away from his ear, someone was driving an iron spike into the wall. The hammer kept slipping, banging and aiming, it seemed, at Sutulin's head. Rubbing his temples, he opened his eyes: the black tube lay in the middle of the narrow table, which had managed somehow to insinuate itself between the bed, the windowsill and the wall. Sutulin tore away the leaden seal, and the cap span off in a spiral. From out of the round aperture came a bitterish gingery smell. The smell made his nostrils flare pleasantly.

"Hmm... Let's try it. Although..."

And, having removed his jacket, the possessor of Quadraturin proceeded to the experiment. Stool up against door, bed into middle of room, table on top of bed. Nudging across the floor a saucer of transparent liquid, its glassy surface gleaming with a slightly yellowish tinge, Sutulin crawled along after it, systematically dipping a handkerchief wound round a pencil into the Quadraturin and daubing the floorboards and patterned wallpaper. The room really was, as that man today had said, a matchbox. But Sutulin worked slowly and carefully, trying not to miss a single corner. This was rather difficult since the liquid really did evaporate in an instant or was absorbed (he couldn't tell which) without leaving even the slightest film; there was only its smell, increasingly pungent and spicy, making his head spin, confounding his fingers and causing his knees, pinned to the floor, to tremble slightly. When he had finished with the floorboards and the bottom of the walls, Sutulin rose to his strangely weak and heavy feet and continued to work standing up. Now and then he had to add a little more of the essence. The tube was gradually emptying. It was already night outside. In the kitchen, to the right, a bolt came crashing down. The apartment was readying for bed. Trying not to make any noise, the experimenter, clutching the last of the essence, climbed up onto the bed and from the bed up onto the tottering table: only the ceiling remained to be quadraturinized. But just then someone banged on the wall with his fist, "What's going on? People are trying to sleep, but he's..."

Turning round at the sound, Sutulin fumbled: the slippery tube spurted out of his hand and landed on the floor. Balancing carefully, Sutulin got down with his already drying brush, but it was too late. The tube was empty, and the rapidly fading spot around it smelled stupefyingly sweet. Grasping at the wall in his exhaustion (to fresh sounds of discontent from the left), he summoned his last bit of strength, put the furniture back where it belonged and, without undressing, fell into bed. A black sleep instantly descended on him from above: both tube and man were empty.

## 2

Two voices began in a whisper. Then by degrees of sonority — from piano to mf, from mf to fff — they cut into Sutulin's sleep.

"Outrageous. I don't want any new tenants popping out from under that skirt of yours... Put up with all that racket?!"

"Can't just dump it in the garbage..."

"I don't want to hear about it. You were told: no dogs, no cats, no children..." at which point there ensued such fff that Sutulin was ripped once and for all from his sleep; unable to part eyelids stitched together with exhaustion, he reached — as was his wont — for the edge of the table on which stood the clock. Then it began. His hand groped for a long time, grappling air: there was no clock and no table. Sutulin opened his eyes at once. In an instant he was sitting up, looking dazedly round the room. The table that usually stood right here, at the head of the bed, had moved off into the middle of a faintly familiar, large but ungainly room.

Everything was the same: the skimpy, threadbare rug that had trailed after the table somewhere up ahead of him, and the photographs, and the stool, and the yellow patterns on the wallpaper. But they were all strangely spread out inside the expanded room cube.

"Quadraturin," thought Sutulin, "is terrific!"

And he immediately set about rearranging the furniture to fit the new space. But nothing worked: the abbreviated rug, when moved back beside the bed, exposed worn, bare floorboards; the table and the stool, pushed by habit against the head of the bed, had disencumbered an empty corner latticed with cobwebs and littered with shreds and tatters, once artfully masked by the corner's own crowdedness and the shadow of the table. With a triumphant, but slightly frightened smile, Sutulin went all round his new, practically squared square, scrutinizing every detail. He noted with displeasure that the room had grown more in some places than in others: an external corner, the angle of which was now obtuse, had made the wall askew; Quadraturin, apparently, did not work as well on internal corners; carefully as Sutulin had applied the essence, the experiment had produced somewhat uneven results.

The apartment was beginning to stir. Out in the corridor, occupants shuffled to and fro. The bathroom door kept banging. Sutulin walked up to the threshold and turned the key to the right. Then, hands clasped behind his back, he tried pacing from corner to corner: it worked. Sutulin laughed with joy. How about that! At last! But then he thought: they may hear my footsteps — through the walls — on the right, on the left, at the back. For a minute he stood stock-still. Then he quickly bent down — his temples had suddenly begun to ache with yesterday's sharp thin pain — and, having removed his boots, gave himself up to the pleasure of a stroll, moving soundlessly about in only his socks.

"May I come in?"

The voice of the landlady. He was on the point of going to the door and unlocking it when he suddenly remembered: he mustn't. "I'm getting dressed. Wait a minute. I'll be right out."

"It's all very well, but it complicates things. Say I lock the door and take the key with me. What about the keyhole? And then there's the window: I'll have to get curtains. Today." The pain in his temples had become thinner and more nagging. Sutulin gathered up his papers in haste. It was time to go to the office. He dressed. Pushed the pain under his cap. And listened at the door: no one there. He quickly opened it. Quickly slipped out. Quickly turned the key. Now.

Waiting patiently in the entrance hall was the landlady.

"I wanted to talk to you about that girl, what's her name. Can you believe it, she's submitted an application to the House Committee saying she's..."

"I've heard. Go on."

"It's nothing to you. No one's going to take your eighty-six square feet away. But put yourself in my..."

"I'm in a hurry," he nodded his cap, and flew down the stairs.

### 3

On his way home from the office, Sutulin paused in front of the window of a furniture dealer: the long curve of a couch, a round extendable table... it would be nice — but how could he carry them in past the eyes and the questions? They would guess, they couldn't help but guess...

He had to limit himself to the purchase of a yard of canary-yellow material (he did, after all, need a curtain). He didn't stop by the cafe: he had no appetite. He needed to get home — it would be easier there: he could reflect, look round and make adjustments at leisure. Having unlocked the door to his room, Sutulin gazed about to see if anyone was looking: they weren't. He walked in. Then he switched on the light and stood there for a long time, his arms spread flat against the wall, his heart beating wildly: *this he had not expected* — not at all.

The Quadraturin was *still* working. During the eight or nine hours Sutulin had been out, it had pushed the walls at least another seven feet apart; the floorboards, stretched by invisible rods, rang out at his first step — like organ pipes. The entire room, distended and monstrously misshapen, was beginning to frighten and torment him. Without taking off his coat, Sutulin sat down on the stool and surveyed his spacious and at the same time oppressive coffin-shaped living box, trying to understand what had caused this unexpected effect. Then he remembered: he hadn't done the ceiling — the essence had run out. His living box was spreading only sideways, without rising even an inch upwards.

"Stop. I have to stop this quadraturinizing thing. Or I'll..." He pressed his palms to his temples and listened: the corrosive pain, lodged under his skull since morning, was still drilling away. Though the windows in the house opposite were dark, Sutulin took cover behind the yellow length of curtain. His head would not stop aching. He quietly undressed, snapped out the light and got into bed. At first he slept, then he was awoken by a feeling of awkwardness. Wrapping the covers more tightly about him, Sutulin again dropped off, and once more an unpleasant sense of mooringlessness interfered with his sleep. He raised himself up on one palm and felt all around him with his free hand: the wall was gone. He struck a match. Um hmm: he blew out the flame and hugged his knees till his elbows cracked. "It's growing, damn it, it's still growing." Clenching his teeth, Sutulin crawled out of bed and, trying not to make any noise, gently edged first the front legs, then the back legs of the bed toward the receding wall. He felt a little shivery. Without turning the light on again, he went to look for his coat on that nail in the corner so as to wrap himself up more warmly. But there was no hook on the wall where it had been yesterday, and he had to feel around for several seconds before his hands chanced upon fur. Twice more during a night that was long and nagging as the pain in his temples, Sutulin pressed his head and knees to the wall as he was falling asleep and, when he awoke, fiddled about with the legs of the bed again. In doing this — mechanically, meekly, lifelessly — he tried, though it was still dark outside, not to open his eyes: it was better that way.

4

Towards dusk the next evening, having served out his day, Sutulin was approaching the door to his room: he did not quicken his step and, upon entering, felt neither consternation nor horror. When the dim, sixteen candle-power bulb lit up somewhere in the distance beneath the long low vault, its yellow rays struggling to reach the dark, ever-receding corners of the vast and dead, yet empty barrack, which only recently, before Quadraturin, had been a cramped but cozy, warm and lived-in cubbyhole, he walked resignedly towards the yellow square of the window, now diminished by perspective; he tried to count his steps. From there, from a bed squeezed pitifully and fearfully in the corner by the window, he stared dully and wearily through deep-boring pain at the swaying shadows nestled against the floorboards, and at the smooth low overhang of the ceiling. "So, something forces its way out of a tube, and can't stop squaring: a square squared, a square of squares squared. I've got to think faster than it: if I don't outthink it, it will outgrow me and..." And suddenly someone was hammering on the door, "Citizen Sutulin, are you in there?"

From the same faraway place came the muffled and barely audible voice of the landlady, "He's in there. Must be asleep."

Sutulin broke into a sweat: "What if I don't get there in time, and they go ahead and..." And, trying not to make a sound (let them think he was asleep), he slowly made his way through the darkness to the door. There.

"Who is it?"

"Oh, open up! Why's the door locked? Re-measuring Commission. We'll remeasure and leave."

Sutulin stood with his ear pressed to the door. Through the thin panel he could hear the clump of heavy boots. Figures were being mentioned, and room numbers.

"This room next. Open up!"

With one hand Sutulin gripped the knob of the electric-light switch and tried to twist it, as one might twist the head of a bird: the switch spattered light, then crackled, spun feebly round and drooped down. Again someone hammered on the door, "Well!"

Sutulin turned the key to the left. A broad black shape squeezed itself into the doorway.

"Turn on the light."

"It's burned out."

Clutching at the door handle with his left hand, and the bundle of wire with his right, he tried to hide the extended space from view. The black mass took a step back.

"Who's got a match? Give me that box. We'll have a look anyway. Do things right."

Suddenly the landlady began whining, "Oh, what is there to look at? Eighty-six square feet for the eighty-sixth time. Measuring the room won't make it any bigger. He's a quiet man, home from a long day at the office — and you won't let him rest: have to measure and remeasure. Whereas other people, who have no right to the space, but..."

"Ain't that the truth," the black mass muttered and, rocking from boot to boot, gently and even almost affectionately drew the door to the light. Sutulin was left alone on wobbling, cottony legs in the middle of the four-cornered, inexorably growing and proliferating darkness.

## 5

He waited until their steps had died away, then quickly dressed and went out. They'd be back, to remeasure or check they hadn't under-measured or whatever. He could finish thinking better here — from crossroad to crossroad. Towards night a wind came up: it rattled the bare frozen branches on the trees, shook the shadows loose, droned in the wires and beat against walls, as if trying to knock them down. Hiding the needle-like pain in his temples from the wind's buffets, Sutulin went on, now diving into the shadows, now plunging into the lamplight. Suddenly, through the wind's rough thrusts, something softly and tenderly brushed against his elbow. He turned round. Beneath feathers batting against a black brim, a familiar face with provocatively half-closed eyes. And barely audible through the moaning air: "You know you know me. And you look right past me. You ought to bow. That's it."

Her slight figure, tossed back by the wind, perched on tenacious stiletto heels, was all insubordination and readiness for battle.

Sutulin tipped his cap. "But you were supposed to be going away. And you're still here? Then something must have prevented..."

"That's right — this."

And he felt a chamois finger touch his chest then dart back into the muff. He sought out the narrow pupils of her eyes beneath the dancing black feathers, and it seemed that one more look, one more touch, one more shock to his hot temples, and it would all come unthought, undone and fall away. Meanwhile she, her face nearing his, said, "Let's go to your place. Like last time. Remember?"

With that, everything stopped.

"That's impossible."

She sought out the arm that had been pulled back and clung to it with tenacious chamois fingers.

"My place... isn't fit," he looked away, having again withdrawn both his arms and the pupils of his eyes.

"You mean to say it's cramped. My God, how silly you are. The more cramped it is..." The wind tore away the end of her phrase. Sutulin did not reply. "Or, perhaps you don't..."

When he reached the turning, he looked back: the woman was still standing there, pressing her muff to her bosom, like a shield; her narrow shoulders were shivering with cold; the wind cynically flicked her skirt and lifted up the lappets of her coat.

"Tomorrow. Everything tomorrow. But now..." And, quickening his pace, Sutulin turned resolutely back.

"Right now: while everyone's asleep. Collect my things (only the necessaries) and go. Run away. Leave the door wide open: let *them*. Why should I be the only one? Why not let *them*?"

The apartment was indeed sleepy and dark. Sutulin walked down the corridor, straight and to the right, opened the door with resolve and, as always, wanted to turn the light switch, but it spun feebly in his fingers, reminding him that the circuit had been broken. This was an annoying obstacle. But it couldn't be helped. Sutulin rummaged in his pockets and found a box of matches: it was almost empty. Good for three or four flares — that's all. He would have to husband both light and time. When he reached the coat pegs, he struck the first match: light crept in yellow radiuses through the black air. Sutulin purposely, overcoming temptation, concentrated on the illuminated scrap of wall and the coats and jackets hanging from hooks. He knew that there, behind his back, the dead, quadraturinized space with its black corners was still spreading. He knew and did not look round. The match smouldered in his left hand, his right pulled things off hooks and flung them on the floor. He needed another flare; looking at the floor, he started towards the corner — if it was still a corner and if it was still there — where, by his calculations, the bed should have fetched up, but he accidentally held the flame under his breath — and again the black wilderness closed in. One last match remained: he struck it over and over: it would not light. One more time — and its crackling head fell off and slipped through his fingers. Then, having turned around, afraid to go any further into the depths, the man started back towards the bundle he had abandoned under the hooks. But he had made the turn, apparently, inexactly. He walked — heel to toe, heel to toe — holding his fingers out in front of him, and found nothing: neither the bundle, nor the hooks, nor even the walls. "I'll get there in the end. I must get there." His body was sticky with cold and sweat. His legs wobbled oddly. The man squatted down, palms on the floorboards: "I shouldn't have come back. Now here I am alone, nowhere to turn." And suddenly it struck him: "I'm waiting here, but it's growing, I'm waiting, but it's..."

In their sleep and in their fear, the occupants of the quadratures adjacent to citizen Sutulin's eighty-six square feet couldn't make head or tail of the timbre and intonation of the cry that woke them in the middle of the night and compelled them to rush to the threshold of the Sutulin cell: for a man who is lost and dying in the wilderness to cry out is both futile and belated: but if even so — against all sense — he does cry out, then, most likely, *thus*.

*1926*

# In the Pupil

## 1

**H**uman love is a frightened thing with half-shut eyes: it dives into the dusk, skitters about dark corners, speaks in whispers, hides behind curtains and puts out the light.

I do not grudge the sun. Let it peek — so long as I too am there too — under the unfastening buttons. Let it peep through the window. That doesn't bother me.

I've always been of the opinion that for a love affair, midday suits far better than midnight. The moon, on which so many rapturous exclamations have been wasted, that night sun beneath a vulgar blue lampshade, I cannot bear. The story of one "yes" and its consequences — to which this narrative is devoted — began in the bright sun, before a window flung wide to the light. I am not to blame if the end surprised her between day and night, in the dim twilight. The one to blame is she, whose "yes" I had so long and passionately awaited.

But even before that "yes" certain events occurred which I must mention here. I can say in all certainty that in love the eyes... now, how shall I put it... always run ahead. That's understandable: they are nimbler and know how to do their part, that is, how to look at and *through*. While the lovers' bodies, huge and clumsy as compared to their eyes, hide behind the stuff of their clothes, while even their words shrink and shilly-shally on their lips, afraid to leap into the air, their eyes — stealing a march on all — are already surrendering.

Oh, how clearly I remember that bright, blue-sky day when we both, standing in the window thrown open to the sun, at once, as if by agreement, looked... not out the window, of course, but at each other. Just then there appeared a *third*: a tiny little man staring at me from out of her pupil, my miniature likeness: he had already slipped in there. I hadn't so much as ruffled her dress, but he... I smiled and nodded to him. The little man nodded back. But then her eyes shied away, and we didn't meet again until that famous "yes".

When it called me, that tiny, barely audible "yes", I did not demur; I took her meek hands in mine, and I saw *him*: leaning out of the round pupil window, *he* was bringing his anxious face closer and closer. Her eyelashes masked him for an instant. Then he reappeared — and again vanished: his face, I noticed, shone with joy and a proud satisfaction; he resembled a capable administrator, fussing and clucking over a client's affairs.

After that, at our every meeting, before seeking out her lips with mine, I would look under my beloved's lashes for him, love's tiny organizer: he was always at his post, neat and punctual, and no matter how tiny the little man's face was in her pupil, I always guessed his expression exactly — now boyishly buoyant, now a bit weary, now quietly contemplative.

One day, at one of our meetings, I told my friend about

the little man who had stolen into her pupil, and my thoughts about him. To my surprise, my story met with coldness and even some hostility.

"What nonsense!" Her pupils jerked away from me instinctively. Then I took her head in my palms and tried to find the little man by force. But she just laughed and lowered her eyelids.

"No, no." In her laughter I also detected non-laughter.

Sometimes you become used to a trifle, invent a meaning for it, philosophize it — and, before you know it, the trifle is rising up, starting arguments with the important and the real, brazenly demanding more existence and legitimacy. I had become rather used to the trifling little man in her pupil; it pleased me to see, when talking of this or that, that both *she and he* were listening. What's more, we fell into the habit of playing a sort of game (who knows what lovers will think up) in which she would hide the little man, and I would look for him: this with a lot of laughter and kisses. Then one day (it still pains me to recall this)... one day, as I brought my lips to hers, I looked into her eyes and saw the little man looking out and waving to me — his expression was sad and circumspect. Then all of a sudden, he turned his back to me and trotted away into the pupil.

"Come on and kiss me!" Her eyelids closed over the little man.

"Stop!" I cried and, forgetting myself, squeezed her shoulders. Frightened, she looked up, and in the depths of her dilated pupil I again glimpsed the tiny figure of the disappearing *me*.

In response to her anxious questions, I said nothing, concealing the truth. I sat there, looking away, and I knew: the game was over.

## 2

For several days I did not show my face — not to her, not to anyone else. Then a letter found me: the narrow cream-colored envelope contained a dozen question marks: Had I had to go away unexpectedly? Was I ill? "Perhaps I am ill," I thought as I reread the crooked cobwebby lines, and I resolved to go to her straightaway. But near the building where my friend lived, I sat down on a bench and began to wait for the dusk. Doubtless, this was cowardice, utterly absurd cowardice: I was afraid, you see, afraid of again not seeing what I had not seen. You would think that then the simplest thing would have been to search her pupils with mine. It was probably just an ordinary hallucination — a figment of the pupil — nothing more. But that's just it — the very act of checking would signify the little man's separate real existence and point to my own mental derangement. The impossibility of this absurd trifle must be — so I then thought -- proved with pure logic, without yielding to the temptation of an experiment: for a series of real actions performed for the sake of someone unreal would lend him a certain reality. My fear, of course, I easily contrived to hide from myself: I was sitting on a bench because the weather was fine, because I was tired, and because the little man in the pupil was not a bad theme for a story and why not consider it here, now, at my leisure, at least in outline? Eventually, the gathering darkness admitted me to her building. In the dusky vestibule I heard "Who's there?" The voice was hers, but a bit *different* or, rather, for a different person.

"Oh, it's you. Finally!"

We went into her room. Her hand, dimly white in the gloaming, reached for the light switch.

"No, don't."

I pulled her to me, and we loved each other without eyes, with a love swathed in darkness. That evening we did not turn on the light. Then we settled on a next meeting and I left, feeling like a man who has received a stay.

I need not go into details: the further one goes, the less interesting it gets. Any man with a smooth gold band on his finger can finish telling this chapter: with our meetings moved from midday to midnight, they became dull, blind and sleepy, like the night. Little by little our love became run-of-the-mill and double-bed, with a lengthy inventory — from soft slippers to chamber pot inclusive. I agreed to everything: fear of happening upon her pupils and finding them empty, without me, woke me every morning, an hour before daylight. I would quietly get up, get dressed, tiptoe to the door, and carefully let myself out. At first these early-morning disappearances struck her as strange. Then they too became habit. Thank you, man with the band on your finger, I'll tell the rest myself. And as I strode home through the city in the chill early dawn, I would invariably reflect on the little man in the pupil. Gradually — from reflection to reflection — the idea of him ceased to frighten me: if before I had feared his real existence and had thought of him with suspicion and alarm, now the little man's nonexistence — his very ghostliness and illusoriness — seemed to me sad.

"How many of them are there, those tiny reflections we scatter about in other people's eyes?" I would wonder as I walked along the blank, deserted streets. "Were I to gather them up, my tiny likenesses in other people's pupils, I would have a small nation of modified, minimized 'I's... They exist, of course, when I look at them, but then so do I exist when someone looks at me. Let that person close his eyes and... What bunk! But if this is bunk, if I am not someone's apparition, but a separate entity, then the little man in the pupil is a separate entity too."

Here my slumberous thoughts usually became entangled, and I would unravel them anew.

"Strange. Why did he go away? And where? Well, all right, suppose her pupils are empty. What of it? Why do I need some tiny personish speck? What do I care whether he exists or not? And how is it that some little pupil man has dared to meddle in my affairs, to illusorize my life, and to separate two people?"

Stuck in that thought, there were times when I was ready to go back on my word, to wake her and to extract the secret from under her eyelid: was he there or not?

But I never returned before evening; and if the light were on in her room, I would avert my face and ignore her caresses. I was certainly sullen and rude till the darkness blindfolded our eyes. Then I would boldly press my face to hers and ask, over and again: Do you love me? And our nighttime ways would take hold.

3

One such night I suddenly felt — through layers of sleep — that something invisible was tugging violently at a lash of my left eyelid. I opened my eyes: something went tumbling head over tiny heels by my left eye, then skidded down my cheek into my ear and cried out in a shrill voice:

"How the deuce! Like an empty apartment in here: not a sound."

"What was that?" I muttered, not sure if I were awake or dreaming.

"Not what, who! That's in the first place. In the second place, press your ear to the pillow so I can jump out. Closer. Closer still. That's it."

On the edge of the pillowcase, palely visible through the gray dawn air, sat the little man from her pupil. Leaning against the white nap, he hung down his head and panted for breath, like a traveler at the end of a long and difficult journey. His face was sad and intent. In his hands he held a black book with gray clasps.

"So you're not an illusion?!" I exclaimed, staring at the little man in amazement.

"What a silly question," he snapped. "And don't make so much noise: we'll wake her up. Bring your ear closer. There. I have something to report."

He stretched out his tired legs, settled himself more comfortably and began in a whisper:

There's no need to tell you how I got into her pupil. We both know all about that. My new premises pleased me: full of glassy reflections, a bow window in a rainbow-colored frame, I found it cozy and cheerful; the convex panes were regularly washed with tears, and at night the blinds came down automatically — in short, an apartment with conveniences. True, there was a long, dark corridor leading who knew where, but I spent almost all of my time at the window, waiting for you. Whatever that was behind my back, I didn't care. Then one day, one of your assignations didn't take place: I paced up and down the corridor, trying not to go too far for fear of missing you. Meanwhile, it was getting dark out the pupil's round aperture. "He won't come," I thought. I began to feel a little bored: not knowing how to amuse myself, I decided to walk to the end of the corridor. But in the pupil, as I said, the light was fading, and after a few steps I found myself in complete darkness. My outstretched hand met nothing but air. I was about to turn back when I heard a soft, stifled sound coming from the depths of the long, narrow passageway. I tried to make it out: it sounded like the chanting of several voices, off-key, but doggedly determined. It even seemed to me that my ear distinguished the words "gallows" and "death". The rest was inaudible.

This phenomenon struck me as curious, but I judged it wiser to return to my post by the window before her lowered eyelid barred my way back with darkness.

But that was not the end. The very next day, without even stirring from my post, I again heard voices behind my back, hymning in frantic cacophony: though the words were still indistinct, it was clear that this choir consisted solely of male voices. This sad circumstance set me thinking. I should

investigate the passageway all the way to the end. I can't
say I especially wanted to do this, given the risks: I might
run into who knew what and lose my way back to the window
and the world. For two or three days I heard no more voices.
"Perhaps I imagined them?" I thought, trying to calm myself.
But then one day, in broad daylight, when the woman and I
had sat down at our respective windows to wait for you, the
phenomenon recurred, this time with surprising intensity and
force: the discordant confusion of words droning and intoning
got inside my ears, and their meaning was such that I firmly
resolved to find the singers. Curiosity and impatience gripped
me. But I didn't want to go away without letting you know:
we waved goodbye — remember? — you seemed somewhat
surprised — then I walked quickly away into the pupil. It
was quiet as quiet. The light, which had streamed after me
for a time down the narrow cave-like passage, gradually
faded. Soon my steps were resounding in the pitch-black. I
went along, grabbing at the passage's slippery walls and
stopping occasionally to listen. Finally, flickering dimly in the
distance, I saw a dead, yellow light: it shone with the
cheerless opacity of a will-o'-the-wisp. I was suddenly
overcome with exhaustion and a blind indifference. "What
was I looking for? What did I need in these catacombs?" I
asked myself. "Why trade the sun for this foul, yellow murk?"
I might well have turned back, but just then the singing, about
which I had almost forgotten, recommenced: now I could
distinguish separate voices poking out of that weird hymn:

*Man-man-man, nimble man, my little man,*
*If you wish your life to keep, ask the pupil before you leap.*

*Odd.*

*Jump into the pupil and you'll know: in the pupil is*

*a gallows —*

*Put your neck in the noose — and expire. Fire with fire.*

*Even.*

*Little man, you mustn't fumble: careful not to take a tumble.*

*Life apart is death to the heart. Days on end all days*

*end in a dead end.*

*Odd-odd.*

*Little man — little-lit-li-l:*

*Now you see him, now you don't. Hark!*

*Even.*

The nonsensicalness pulled me along, as a hook does a fish. Fast approaching was a round opening, the source of the yellow light. I grasped the edges of the hole and stuck my head inside: from the emptiness below a dozen gullets howled; the yellow luminescence dazzled my eyes. Peering about, I leaned over the precipice, but just then the aperture's slippery sides slid apart and, helplessly grappling air, I went crashing down. It wasn't far to the bottom; I sat up and looked round. As my eyes adjusted to the light, they began to see: I was sitting inside what appeared to be an opaque glass bottle with pulsating sides, exactly in the center of its cambered bottom. Under me a yellow smudge was oozing light, around me some ten human shapes half hidden in shadow — soles to the glow, heads to the wall — were finishing their solemn refrain:

*Little man, little-lit-li-l:*

*Now you see him, now you don't. Hark!*

*Even.*

My question — "Where am I?" — vanished into the wails. Looking for a way out, I stood up on my convex perch only to lose my footing, topple down the incline and — to roars of delighted laughter — land on my backside between two of the well's inmates.

"Getting too crowded around here," the man on my left grumbled and moved over. But the man on my right turned to me with a look of compassion. His face was, I would say, of the university-lecturer type: a knobby erudite forehead, thoughtful eyes, a Vandyke beard and hair combed carefully over a bald pate.

"Who are you all? And where am I?"

"We... are your predecessors. Don't you see? A woman's pupil is like any other premises: first they take you in, then they boot you out: and everyone winds up here. I, for instance, am Sixth; that man, on your left, is Second. You're Twelfth. True, we don't go strictly by numbers, but in order of associations. Got it? Or must put it more crudely? Besides... you may have hit your head."

"Against the wall?"

"No: against the meaning."

For a minute we neither of us said anything.

"By the way: don't forget to register your having been forgotten. Oh, these women's pupils," he said, fingering his beard, "pupils inviting us under a canopy of lashes. To think: such a marvelous entrance, bathed in rainbow shimmers, and such a dark vile bottom. There was a time when I too..."

I interrupted:

"Who registers you?"

"Quagga."

"I've never heard of such a name."

"Well, have you heard of telegony?"

"No."

"Hmm... then you probably know nothing about Lord Morton's mare."

"What's that got to do with...?"

"Everything: there was a mare, that is, beg pardon, first there was Lord Morton. His mare produced a striped foal sired by Quagga, then Lord Morton produced the theory of telegony inspired by Quagga and his mare: you see, regardless of the sire, the mare's offspring were always striped — in memory, so to speak, of Quagga, who was her first. Hence the conclusion that the female's bond with *her* first is *never-ending* and lives on, as it were, in her subsequent bonds, indelibly and ineradicably. The first inmate of the pupil, on the bottom of which you and I now sit, has laid claim, since chronology is on his side, to the role of Quagga. True, I've told him countless times that Mr. Ewart disproved this theory long ago, but still he insists on playing the dictator. He claims that he is the soil, and we are mere pumps, and that all our attempts to repeat the unrepeatable..."

"Tell me," I asked, "has this telegony, or whatever it's called, really been definitively disproved, or...?"

"I knew it," the university lecturer smiled. "I've noticed this before: the higher the number, the greater the interest in the question: Is love striped or not? But let's discuss that later. Listen: First is calling you."

"Forgotten No. 12, come here!"

I got up and, sliding my palms along the wall, went towards the voice. As I stepped over the legs strewn in my path, I noticed that I could see some of the pupil's inmates more clearly than others: some so blended with the yellow gloom of those lower depths that I tripped over them without meaning to, without noticing their faded, partially effaced shapes. Suddenly two invisible hands took a firm grip of my ankles.

"Please answer these questions."

I bent down to look at the hands shackling me, but they were not to be seen: No. 1 had become so thoroughly discolored that he was now the color of air. His invisible fingers let go of me and clicked open the clasps of a book. This book right here. Filled-out pages rose and fell, and rose again, until there appeared an empty page with my number on it.

The form ran to dozens of questions: it began with your date of moving in, reasons for doing so, expected length of stay (opposite this item were suggested answers — a) for all eternity, b) until death, c) until I find something better — and instructions to "underline the correct one"); it ended, as I recall, with a list of pet names and diminutives and your attitude towards jealousy. I quickly filled out my page. An invisible finger folded it back to reveal white sheets gleaming blankly.

"So then," said Quagga, closing the book, "one more late-lamented; the book is slowly filling up. That's all. You may go."

I went back to my place between Second and Sixth.

Sixth's whitish beard wanted to intrude, but, meeting with silence, shrank into the shadows.

I sat there for a long time plunged in my thoughts about the registry book's blank pages. A sudden noise brought me back to reality.

"Eleventh, into the middle," Quagga's voice shouted.

"Eleventh, Eleventh," echoed from all sides.

"What's this?" I turned to my neighbor.

"The same old story," he said, "in numerical order: so next time it'll be your turn..."

There was no need to ask any more questions since Eleventh was already clambering up onto the hump. His cumbrous shape looked immediately familiar. My predecessor sat down on the yellow smudge and peered calmly about. He caught the ribbon dangling from his pince-nez in his lips and worried it meditatively, causing his flaccid cheeks to jiggle:

"Yes indeed. It's funny to recall, but there was a time when, like each of you, I had only one aim in life. And that was — somehow or other, by hook or by crook — to steal into our mistress' pupil. So here we all are. What else is there to say?"

He wound the pince-nez ribbon round his finger, pulled the lenses off his nose and, screwing up his eyes with an air of disgust, went on:

"A mantrap. That's what it is. But I'll stick to the point. Our first meeting decided everything. That day, I remember, she wore a black buttoned-up dress. Her face, too, seemed tightly buttoned-up, her lips were sternly pursed, her eyes half shut. The cause of her melancholy now sits on my left:

our respected Tenth. His story, which we heard last time, is fresh in all our memories: the forgotten do not forget. But at the time I didn't yet have the honor of knowing him. Still, I guessed that in the pupils hiding under her lashes all was not well. And indeed, when I finally managed to look into her eyes, I saw such abandonedness that I — who had been on the lookout for pupils to suit — decided there and then to occupy those empty premises.

"But how was I to do this? Everyone has his own way of winning a person's heart. Mine is to perform all manner of minor, preferably inexpensive services: 'Have you read such-and-such by so-and-so?' — 'No, but I'd like to...' Next morning a messenger delivers an uncut copy of the book. The eyes, into which you wish to steal, discover a touching inscription over your name inside the cover. The tip of a hatpin has gone missing, or the needle for cleaning the primus: make it your business to remember all this piffle so that at your next meeting you may, smirking devotedly, pluck out of your vest pocket a primus needle, a hatpin tip, a ticket to the opera, aspirin in capsules, and who knows what else. For, you see, one person can penetrate another only in tiny doses, with little, barely visible men who, once they have accumulated in sufficient number, capture the consciousness. Among them will be one, as pitifully tiny as the others, but if he disappears, so will the meaning. All that atomism will disintegrate, instantly and irrevocably: but I needn't explain this to you, my fellow inmates.

"So then, I set my system of minor services in motion: everywhere among the baubles, books, and pictures amassed on the walls of the room in which our mistress lived, my agents began appearing. Her eyes could not escape these little men who had slipped into every corner and who, from every cranny, whispered my name. Sooner or later, I mused, one of them will squeeze his way through into her pupil. But for now, work was proceeding slowly: her eyelids, as if they weighed God knows how much, rarely yielded, which for me, a man from the pupil, made the situation very difficult.

"I remember that in response to my umpteenth service she smiled to herself and said:

"'I believe you're courting me. You're wasting your time.'

"'I don't care,' I replied meekly. 'Halfway to the Crimean coast, I once glanced out the train window at a stop and saw a brick hovel slumped among yellow patches of fields; on the hovel was a sign, and on the sign the name of the station: Patience.'

"Her eyes opened slightly.

"'So you think this is the halfway mark, do you? That's amusing.'

"I can't remember what silly thing I said in reply, but I do remember that the train, when it reached Patience, stopped there too long. I then resolved to resort to your aid, my kind predecessors. I didn't know who you were, or how many, but I instinctively felt that her pupils were, so to speak, lived-in, that several Xs of the male sex hung over them, that their reflections... In short, I decided, having plunged my spoon into the past, to the bottom, to stir it up again. If a woman *no longer* loves one man and hasn't *yet* fallen in love with another, then *yet*, if he has any sense at all, must shake *no longer* — shake him and shake him — until *no longer* shows him all the approaches and means of access.

"I used my spoon approximately thus: 'Women don't love men like me. I know that. The man you loved wasn't like me. Am I right? Man or men? You won't say? Well, of course. It was probably...' And with the dull-witted zeal of a worker charged with stirring a mash, I continued to revolve my questions. At first they met with silence, then mono-syllables. I could see on the surface of her consciousness, rising from the bottom, bubbles beginning to swell and burst, flashing iridescences that had seemed forever buried in the past. Heartened by my success, I went on with my task of stirring. I knew very well that you couldn't disturb emotional stimuli without disturbing the emotion itself. The rejected images, raised from the depths, sank back down into the darkness, but the remnants of the feeling they brought up with them would not subside and went on clinging to the surface. More and more often her eyes rose to meet my questions. Any number of times, I bent my knees, preparing to jump... But my enormous likeness, in whose pupil I then resided, owing to his clumsiness and cumbrousness, missed one chance after another. Finally, the fateful day arrived: I, rather we, found her by the window, her shoulders shivering under a warm shawl.

"'What's the matter with you?'

"'Nothing. I have a fever. Don't take any notice.'

"But the man who is wedded to the method of minor services must take notice. I flew out the door, and a quarter of an hour later was told to:

"'Turn around.'

"Staring fixedly at the minute hand on my watch, I heard silk rustle and a snap unsnap: the thermometer was being tucked into the proper place.

"'Well?'

"'98.6.'

"At that point, not even my absurd blunderbuss could fail to make the correct diagnosis. We moved closer to her.

"'You don't know how. Allow me.'

"'Leave me alone.'

"'First give it a good shake. Like that. And then...'

"'Don't you dare!'

"Now their eyes were close together. I positioned myself — and jumped: her pupils shone with that misty patina, the surest possible sign... But I had misjudged the distance and found myself caught on the curve of an eyelash that was batting about like a branch in a storm. I know my business, though, and a few seconds later I was climbing inside her pupil, agitated and out of breath. Behind me I heard first the sound of a kiss, then the tinkle of the thermometer on the floor. Then her eyelids slammed shut. But I am not curious. Feeling that I had done my duty, I sat down under the round vault and reflected on the difficult and dangerous profession of the little man in the pupil: the future proved me right. More than right: for it turned out to be even more dismal than my most dismal imaginings."

Eleventh fell silent and drooped dejectedly from the glowing rise. The forgotten ones again began to sing — at first quietly, then louder and louder — their strange hymn:

*Man-man-man, nimble man, my little man,*
*If you wish your life to keep, ask the pupil before you leap,*
*Odd-odd.*

"What a brazen beast," I summed up on meeting Sixth's inquiring look.

"He's an odd number. They're all like that."

I said I didn't understand.

"Why yes. Haven't you noticed? Here am I, Sixth, on one side of you, while Second and Fourth are on the other. We even numbers stick together because all those odd numbers — as though handpicked — are boors and bullies. Whereas we, calm and civilized people..."

"But how do you explain that?"

"How? How shall I put it... the heart, no doubt, has its own rhythms, or changing desires, a sort of dialectic of love that alternates thesis and antithesis, boors and gentlemen like you and me."

Sixth chuckled good-naturedly and winked. But I didn't feel like laughing. Then he too stopped smiling.

"You see," he said, moving closer to me, "you mustn't rush to judge: it's the audience that creates the speaker's style. You'll soon see this for yourself. You can't deny that Eleventh is observant. Put it this way: people use diminutives to express augmentative emotional processes; the significance grows — the sign diminishes. We call those who mean *more* to us than others by diminutive names; it's no wonder that in Old Church Slavonic the words *mil** and *mal*** were

---

* Dear (*OCS*).
** Small *(OCS)*.

confused. Yes, like Eleventh, I am convinced that women love not those great mastodons by whom we are propelled from pupil to pupil, but us, the itinerant little men, who spend their lives cooped up in other people's eyes. And if one discounts the commonness of his system of minor services, then here too Eleventh is right: to seduce is to take possession of the 'associative mass' of the one seduced; what's more, love itself, schematically speaking, is nothing but a special case of *two-way association...*"

"What on earth...?"

"Here's what: in classifying our associations, psychologists have failed to notice that the connection between mental pictures is either one-way or two-way... Wait a minute," he sputtered, noticing my gesture of impatience, "a minute of boredom, and then it gets interesting — you'll see. The seducer, of course, combines not an idea and an image, not an image and a concept, but an image (the person) and an emotion; he must remember that this process goes from emotions to image, or from image to emotion. And until that double spark, if you will, is produced, until... What? Not clear? Well think about it. I can't very well think for you. Examples? Certainly. First case: the emotion is present, but as yet undirected, unassociated with an image; at the outset you have 'a soul waiting for someone', agitation with no object, firing into air. Then the 'some' falls away — at that point, it is extremely easy to fill the vacant 'one'. Second case: when the image has to wait for the emotion: here the coalescence of associative elements may be slow and difficult. Love affairs in one's first youth most often take the first route, in one's second youth, the second. But the law of associations causes lovers a lot of trouble: given a constant love, the "beloved", every time he or she walks into the room, must inspire — by association — a feeling of love; by the same token, all sexual excitement should call up the image of that same 'beloved'. But in reality, the feeling and the image are usually connected like the currents of a cathode circuit when hooked up to a rectifier, that is, they only go one way. Most relationships are based on these one-way half-loves: in the first type of relationship, the associative current runs from image to emotion, but not vice versa; this makes for a maximum of infidelities, but a fine passion. Why? My God, he doesn't understand anything! Well, instead of the rectifier connection, let's take the circulation of the blood through the heart: flowing in one direction, the blood opens the valves; flowing in the other, it closes them, thus barring the way to itself. The same is true here: every meeting is passionate, indeed, every thought that enters the consciousness, every image in this case, causes a rush of passionate feeling — the blood, if you will, opens the valves for itself; but this emotion, when it arises in the absence of the image medium, is easily channeled elsewhere; people who fall in love in this manner are in love only during encounters, the image of the loved one quickly finds the way to the feeling, but that feeling does not know the way to the loved one, the blood, flowing towards love, closes the heart valves to itself. That, I think, was a yawn. Nervous? Now. The second type of falling in love yields, please note, a small percent of infidelities, but a passion that is weak: an attack of love hunger invariably calls up in the consciousness — both during encounters and not — one and the same image, but that image, if it enters the consciousness, doesn't pull the emotion after it: this sort of one-way associatedness works very well for daily relations, it is familial and averse to dramas. But only the third type — two-way association, when image and emotion are inseparable — yields what I would agree to call love. Say what you like, Eleventh knows where the truth lies, but he doesn't know how to get at it. Whereas I..."

"Why dig up all that rot," I scowled.

For a minute Sixth sat silent. His face wore the expression of a man intent on mending the broken thread of his thought.

"Because the point which Eleventh reached, but at which he stopped, is the fundamental question for those who, like you and I, have ended up in this black pit of a pupil and... What do we have to hide? We're all sick with a strange chronic colorlessness; time slides over us like an eraser over lines written in pencil, we are perishing like waves in a calm. Fading more and more, I shall soon cease to distinguish the shades of my thoughts, I will lose my contours and vanish into naught. But it's not so much that that I regret, it's that so many observations, scientific facts and formulas shall perish with me. Were I to find my way out of here, I'd show all those Freuds, Adlers and Mayers the true nature of oblivion. What could those smug collectors of slips of the tongue and pen possibly find to say to a man come back from a black pit whose very name is: oblivion. That's not likely though: easier to come back from death than from here. But it would be amusing. From a very young age, you see, I have devoted all my thoughts to the problem of oblivion. My first encounter with it came about almost by accident. I was leafing through a slim volume of poetry when suddenly:

> *Past the flight of birds, a layer of dust,*
> *The disc of the sun sinks spent,*
> *If I'm forgotten then it must*
> *Be now, this very moment.*

"Brooding over this handful of words, I did not suspect that having entered the thought, I would never come out of it again. Ideas, I then reasoned, constantly migrate from the consciousness to the unconscious and back again. But sometimes they go so far into the unconscious that they can't find their way back to the consciousness. How, I began to wonder, does an idea perish? Does it go out like a smoldering ember or like a candle in the wind? Gradually or instantly? After a long and serious illness or suddenly? At first I agreed with the poet: I imagined the process of oblivion to be a long-in-the-making, but instantaneous collapse: now you see it — now you don't. Using Ebbinghaus's mnemonic series, I remember I even tried to determine the moment when this or that idea disappeared, fell away, disintegrated. My attention was immediately drawn to the question of forgotten emotions. A curious question indeed: a certain woman meets with a certain man $n$ times, and every time both experience a nervous excitement; yet at the $n + 1$ meeting the same woman visits the same man, but the nervous excitement does not; the man feigns it as best he can and, when the woman has gone, ransacks his soul in search of what he has lost. In vain: to recall an image that has gone is possible, but to recall a feeling, once it's gone, is utterly impossible: the lizard, if you will, has run away leaving its tail in your hand, the image and the emotion have been dissociated. In studying the cooling process that makes what is dear hateful, I could not resist certain analogies: the cooling of passion, it seemed to me, clearly had something in common with, say, the cooling of a piece of ordinary sulfur. In depriving sulfur of calories, we convert its crystals from one system to another, that is, we force it to change its form, to assume another appearance; moreover, it has been proven that a chemical substance — phosphorus, for instance — when gradually cooled, not only changes its crystalline form and color, turning from violet to red, from red to black, but also — at a certain point in the cooling — loses all shape, decrystallizes, becomes amorphous. Well I wanted to catch the actual moment of deformation... For if one can observe the second when the sparkling carbon we call a diamond changes into the ordinary coal that leaves our hands black, why can't one observe the instant when "I love" turns into...

"But even in the realm of chemical symbols, this was not easy to do: before changing shape, losing its facets and becoming a formless, amorphous substance, the crystal goes through a stage called *metastability* — something halfway between form and formlessness. This analogy struck me as convincing: the relations of many, many people are just that — metastable — somewhere in the middle between ice melting and the boiling point; curiously, metastability has the highest coefficient of resilience. One can take these analogies further. An incandescent substance, if left alone, will cool naturally and continually; the same is true of emotion. Only by changing its objects, only by throwing more and more wood onto the fire of feeling can one maintain its white-hot temperature. Here I remember thinking that these analogies had led me into an impossible impasse. But science, which tells us in which cases temperature cooling turns a crystal into an amorphous something, told me, as it were, in which cases the process of natural emotional cooling turns diamonds into coal, love into indifference, form into formlessness. It appears that a crystalline substance, when subjected to cooling, tends not to lose its form, but merely to *change* it, but since the rate of cooling exceeds that of recrystallization, the latter process hasn't time to take place, and the particles, overcome halfway (between one form and another) by the cold, come to a standstill: the result is frozen and featureless or, to translate chemisms into psychisms, hateful and forgotten. In these conditions, a long and stable relationship can only be this: a succession of betrayals of each other with each other. What are you staring at? That's just what it is: if even one person were absolutely faithful to the image etched in his mind, like an engraving on a copper plate, then that love might last, well, a day or two — at most. For the real love object is constantly changing, and to love you today is to betray the person you were yesterday. You know, if I were a writer, I'd try my hand at this fantastical story: my hero meets a girl, a lovely young creature, not yet eighteen. Fine. They fall in love. Have children. The years go by. Their love remains what it was: strong, good, simple.

Of course, by now he has asthma, she has crow's feet and slack skin. But it's all dear, familiar, their own. Then one day: the door opens and in she walks, only she is not she or, rather, not who she was an hour or a day ago, but her former seventeen-year-old self, the one he vowed to love always and faithfully. My hero is confused and, I imagine, stunned. The visitant stares with incredulity at this foreign, middle-aged life. Her children not born of her. The flabby, half-familiar man who keeps glancing nervously at the door: what if the other woman, the same woman, should walk in? 'Yesterday you promised me,' says the young creature, but the asthmatic scratches his head, unable to understand: 'yesterday' — that was twenty years ago. He feels muddled and doesn't know what to do with his guest. Just then he hears someone coming, the other woman, the same woman now.

"'You have to go, if she finds you here...'

"'Who?'

"'You. Please hurry...'

"But it's too late. The door opens, and my hero, well, let's say... he wakes up..."

"Listen, Sixth, you can't do that: jumping from psychology to chemistry, from chemistry to fiction. And from there I don't see how you'll get back to your crystallization of whatever it was — images or phosphorus and coal."

"But I will get back to that. Listen: someone loves a certain A. But today's A is $A_1$ the next day, and a week later $A_2$. To keep up with this constantly recrystallizing being, one must constantly readjust the image, that is, redirect the emotion from one mental picture to another; from stepping-stone to stepping-stone; betraying A-prime with A-second, and A... And if this series of betrayals, caused by the lovers' variability, proceeds at the same rate as the changes in the beloved, then everything is, so to speak, as it should be — and just as the man out for a stroll will walk a hundred paces without realizing that his body has fallen a hundred times, and been caught each time in time by his muscles, so lovers of several weeks or even years never suspect that *the number of meetings is equal to the number of betrayals.*"

He concluded with the air of a popular speaker expecting applause. But too much theorizing has a soporific effect on me. Sixth said nothing for a minute then again began harping away at the difference in rates, betrayal unable to keep pace with change, change lagging behind betrayal... Unable to keep my eyes open, I sank into a deep sleep. Even there I was pursued by swirling swarms of chemical signs and algebraic symbols: buzzing shrilly, they were angrily embarked on their nuptial flight.

I don't know how long I might have slept if jabs and voices had not awoken me:

"Twelfth, into the middle."

"Now we'll hear from the new boy."

"Twelfth..."

I had no choice. Nudged and nagged right and left, I scrambled up onto the glowing yellow rise. Ten-odd pairs of eyes, squinting at me out of the darkness, prepared to absorb and appropriate the secret of two people. And I began my story: the story that you know. Skip it. When I had finished, they began singing their strange hymn. A dull longing gripped my temples and, rocking from side to side, empty and dead, I sang with them:

> *Put your neck in the noose — and expire. Fire with fire. Even.*

Finally, they let me to go back to my place. I slipped quickly into the shadows. I was shivering so my teeth chattered. Rarely have I felt so vile. His beard nodding in sympathy, Sixth leaned towards me and whispered:

"Forget it. It's not worth it. You've said your piece and that's that. But you do seem undone."

His stiff fingers gave my hand a brief squeeze.

"Listen," I turned to Sixth, "this may be fine for us, myself and the others, but what do you need from love? What are you doing here at the bottom of the pupil? You have the soul of a bibliophile. All you need are your bookmarks. You should have stayed with them and your formulas, your nose in a book, rather than meddling in other people's affairs and getting involved in what doesn't concern you."

The university lecturer looked crestfallen:

"It can happen to anyone, you see... Even Thales, they say, when he was walking along staring up at the stars, once fell into a well. And so did I. I certainly didn't mean to, but if someone trips you with their pupils... I was teaching psychology at the time at the college for women. Seminars, tutorials, papers, what have you. Naturally, my students came to see me, sometimes at home, about this and that — topics, references, sources. She among them. Once, twice. I hadn't yet realized that for a woman, science, like everything else, is personified. Questions — answers — and again questions. I won't say that she was especially gifted. One day, as I was explaining stimulus logarithms in the Weber-Fechner law, I noticed she wasn't listening. 'Repeat what I just said.' She just sat there, looking down and smiling at something. 'I don't know why you bother to come here!' I exploded and, I believe, banged the book on the desk. Then she looked up, and I saw tears in her eyes. I don't know what people do in such cases. I moved closer and made the mistake of looking into her moist pupils. That's when I..."

With a dismissive wave of his hand, Sixth fell silent.

Again the well's yellow murk closed over us. I scanned the glassy walls, cylindrical and seamless, and thought: can this really be my final resting place? Have I really been deprived of the present forever and irrevocably?

Now it was First's turn to speak. Over the yellow smudge lay a black one. Beside it was this book (Quagga always had it with him).

"Given intimacy," the black smudge began, "all women can be divided into four categories. In the first are those who, having agreed to an assignation, allow themselves to be dressed and undressed. This type includes many courtesans of the first water as well as women accomplished in the art of turning their lovers into meek slaves charged with all the responsibility and feverish work of fastening and unfastening hooks and recalcitrant buttons. These women play no part; they close their eyes and merely give leave. The second category consists of the women one undresses, but who dress themselves. The man meanwhile sits staring out the window or at the wall, or smokes a cigarette. To the third category — perhaps the most dangerous — belong the women who guide you to the hooks and buttons themselves, but afterwards make you serve them lovingly in all the touching details of their toilet. These are mostly malicious flirts fond of ambiguous conversations, experienced predators, in a word, the come-hither type. Finally, the fourth category — women who dress and undress themselves independently while their partners wait more or less patiently — is for ruble prostitutes, faded wives and god knows who else. Now I have a question for you: to which category, my good successors, does our mistress belong?"

The smudge paused, only to be accosted on all sides by shouts:

"To the first, of course."

"What are you talking about? To the second!"

"Wrong! To the third!"

Drowning them out, someone's husky bass bellowed:

"To the last of the last."

The black smudge twitched with soundless laughter.

"I knew it: your opinions couldn't help but differ. This book — the one I have in my hands — knows much and about many. True, it has plenty of blank pages left and we're not all here yet. But sooner or later our mistress' pupils will lose their ability to attract and entice. And then, having registered the last of us, I shall compile a *Complete and Systematic History of One Enchantress*. With a subject index and an index of names. My categories are only an outline, for methodological purposes, as Sixth would say. The doors — from category to category — are wide open. It's not surprising that *she* went through them all.

"As you all know, it was with me that she became a woman. The year was... Actually, the only important thing is that it *was*. We were introduced at a literary tea: 'She's new to Moscow, from the provinces, please be kind to her.' Her stiff, unfashionable suit confirmed her provenance. I tried to catch her eyes with mine, but no — lashes fluttering, they broke away.

Later, as we sat stirring our glasses of tea, someone recited something and kept mixing the pages up. The instigator of this cultural tedium took me aside and asked me to see the provincial girl home: she's all alone, you know, it's dark out, she'll become lost. I remember that the loop inside the collar of her coat had been torn off.

We walked out. Into a downpour. I hailed a coachman, and through the pelting rain we dove under the leather hood of his horse-drawn cab. She said something, but the cobbles had already begun to clatter under us and I didn't catch a word. One turn, another turn. I gave her elbow a cautious squeeze: she flinched and tried to move away, but there was nowhere to move. Rogue cobblestones kept throwing us together with short, nervous jolts. Here, somewhere, beside me, in the darkness, were her lips: I wanted to know where exactly, I leaned over — and in that same instant she did something I hadn't expected. She lurched forward, ripped back the leather apron and leapt out of the moving cab. I remember reading of a similar trick in someone's novels, except that there it was typically performed by men, and driving rain did not enter the picture. For several seconds I sat beside emptiness, utterly discouraged and abashed, it took as much more time to rouse the coachman and stop his nag. Seeing me jump out of the cab, the driver balked and began shouting about the fare: another several seconds lost. Finally, I rushed off along the wet pavement, hoping to discern my runaway's silhouette in the blackness of the night. The streetlamps had been doused. At a crossroads I thought I'd caught up with her; she turned round and, a cigarette glowing between her teeth, called: "Come to bed." A harlot. I rushed on. Another crossroads — a confusion of streets: nowhere. Close to despair, I crossed a street at random and ran right into my runaway; she was standing there, shivering and rain-lashed, lost in the maze and not knowing which way to go. I won't recount our conversation: you've heard it many times. My remorse was genuine: kissing her wet fingers, I begged her to forgive me and threatened to kneel down in a puddle if she wouldn't stop being angry. We found another cab and, no matter how the cobbles jostled me, I sat quietly the whole way and kept shifting my shoulder away from hers. We were both numb with cold and our teeth were chattering. As we said goodbye, I again kissed her frozen fingers and suddenly she dissolved in girlish laughter. A day or two later, I called on her with heaps of assurances and patent powders. These latter proved useful: the poor thing had a cough and was complaining of fever. I did not resort to your method, Eleventh. At the time, it was still... too soon. The slightest indiscretion could easily have destroyed our incipient friendship. At the time, I amounted to more than the faded, gray smudge you see before you. Sitting on her sofa's shuddering springs, we often talked until evening. This inexperienced girl knew nothing about the city, about the world, about me. Our conversations, as though buffeted by the wind, bucketed this way and that: first I would patiently explain how to use the kerosene stove, then, a little mixed up myself, I would expound the premises of Kant's critique. Curled up in a corner of the sofa, she listened avidly to what I said — about kerosene stoves, about Kant — without taking her deep dark eyes off me. There was one other thing she knew nothing about: herself. In one of those conversations that drifted into the dusk I tried to explain her to herself, to unfasten the clasps of the tattered, half-filled book here in my hands. That evening we talked of her future, of the encounters, the passions, the dis-appointments and still other encounters. I kept knocking on the door of her future. Now she would give a dry laugh, now she would correct me, now she would listen in silence without interrupting. I happened (my cigarette must have gone out) to strike a match, and in its yellow light I noticed that her face was *different*, older and more womanly, like a vision from the future. I blew out the match and raced ahead in time: her first love, life's first blows, the bitter taste of separations. Then affairs of the heart would be left behind. Rattling on, I was fast approaching the years when feelings are tired and spent, when fear of fading causes one to hurry and rush through happiness, when curiosity gets the better of passion, when... Here I again struck a match and stared amazed into her eyes till I burned my fingers. Yes, my worthy successors, had I done my experiment correctly, a dozen sulfur matches would have shown me the dozen faces carried off by you. But she grabbed the matchbox out of my hands and cast it aside. Our fingers entwined and then started to tremble as though lashed by a cold rain. I don't think I need continue."

The hazy humanoid smudge began its slow descent.

"Well, how do you like Quagga?" asked Sixth.

I rudely said nothing.

"Oh, I suppose you're jealous. I have to admit there was a time when Quagga's claims, his crowing about being first, irritated even me. But you can't throw off the past: it is the king of kings. You have to make your peace with it. And besides, if you think about it, what is jealousy?"

I turned my back on his lecture and pretended to sleep. Sixth muttered something about discourteous people and sank into an offended silence.

At first I feigned sleep, but then I really did drop off. I don't know for how long: a bright light seeped under my lids and forced me to open my eyes. I was bathed in a phosphorescent blue. I raised myself up on one elbow, looking for the source of that strange luminescence. To my astonishment, I found that the light was coming from me: my body was swathed in a phosphorescent nimbus whose abbreviated rays vanished within a few feet. I felt light and springy — the way one does sometimes in dreams. The others were all asleep. I leapt up onto the glowing yellow rise, and our two luminescences, rays crisscrossing, filled the air with rainbows. Another exertion, and my light body, dreamily gliding, began to scale the wall to the vault of the cave. The crack in the vault opened; I gripped the edges and my body, supple and elastic, passed out. Before me stretched the low passageway that had lured me to the bottom. Once before I had roamed its zags, bumping into walls and darkness. But now the gleaming blue light pointed the way. Hope stirred in me as I strode in my phosphorescent sheath towards the pupil's egress. Along the walls, shapes and flecks of light danced ahead of me, but I hadn't time to study them. My heart was pounding in my throat when I finally reached the pupil's round window. Finally! I rushed forward and cannoned violently into her lowered eyelid. That accursed leathern shutter was blocking the exit. I took a swing at it, but it didn't even twitch: she was clearly sound asleep. Furious, I began pummeling the screen with my knees and shoulders. The eyelid fluttered and then the light enveloping me began to dim and fade. In my panic, I rushed back down the passage, afraid of being stranded in the pitch dark; the rays were drawing back into my body, and I could feel my weight returning; leadfooted and gasping for breath, I finally reached the opening in the cave's vault: it meekly expanded and I jumped down. My thoughts were swirling about like grains in a sandstorm: why had I returned? What force had hurled me back to the bottom, from freedom into slavery? Or perhaps this was an absurd nightmare? But then why... I crept back to my place and shook Sixth by the shoulder; he sprang awake and, rubbing his eyes, took the full fire of my questions.

"Just a minute, a dream, you say," he was staring at the last faint flickers of my dying nimbus. "Hmm... A dream may indeed be in progress, and that dream (only don't be surprised) is you. Yes. This has happened to others as well: her dreams sometimes wake us and force us to roam about, like sleepwalkers, without knowing why or where. She's having a dream about you, you see. Look, here you're still shining. Oh, but now it's gone out. That means the dream is over."

"Sixth," I whispered, grabbing his arm, "I can't go on like this. Let's run away."

He shook his head:

"It can't be done."

"But why? I was just there, at the entrance to the world. If not for her eyelid..."

"It can't be done," Sixth said again. "In the first place, who's to guarantee that once you've gotten out of her eye, you'll find your master? They may have separated, the space is huge, and you... you'll lose your way and die. In the second place, other daredevils before you have attempted to escape. They..."

"They what?"

"Came back, that's what."

"Came back?"

"Yes. You see the crack in the vault opens only for those being dreamed about and for those arrived from the outside world. But dreams won't let us go: they bar us from reality with lowered eyelids then hurl us back to the bottom when they've done. There is one other solution: to wait for the crack to open to admit a new arrival and leap out — then follow the dark passages (you know them) to freedom. It sounds simple. But one matter brings it all to naught.

"I don't understand."

"You see, as you are passing out, you will necessarily meet — head to head, shoulder to shoulder — the new man jumping down in your place, into the cave. The temptation to glimpse one's successor, if only for an instant, is usually so strong... In short, lose that instant, and you lose your freedom: the crack seals shut, and you both fall down to the bottom. That, at any rate, was the fate of all previous attempts. Here you have a psychological trap that no one can resist."

I listened in silence, and the more Sixth said, "it can't be done", the more determined I became.

I spent several hours mapping out a detailed plan. Meanwhile, Second's turn had come. My taciturn neighbor crept out into the yellow light. I saw for the first time his discolored form, drab and hunched. With an embarrassed cough, he began, stammering slightly:

"It happened this way. One day I received a letter in a long envelope. It smelled faintly of verbena. I opened it: slanting cobwebby script. And began to read: what's wrong?"

"Shhhh!" Quagga's voice rang out. "Stop the story. Up there... Hear?"

The storyteller and extraneous voices fell silent. At first I heard nothing. But then, from somewhere far overhead, came the sound (real? — imagined?) of soft, cautious footsteps. It stopped. Started. Stopped again.

"Did you hear that?" Sixth whispered in my ear. "He's come. He's roaming."

"Who?"

"Thirteenth."

And we began to sing — softly at first, so as not to scare him away, then louder and louder — our hymn of the forgotten. From time to time, at a sign from Quagga, we would stop singing and listen. The footsteps, which had seemed to be coming closer, suddenly began to recede.

"Louder now, louder!" Quagga shouted. "Lure him in, lure him. You won't get away, my friend, oh no-o-o-o."

Our hoarse voices, straining to fever pitch, beat against the slimy walls of our prison.

But Thirteenth, unseen in the dark aisles above, couldn't make up his mind and kept retracing his steps. We sang till we could sing no more. Quagga allowed us to rest, and soon everyone had fallen asleep.

I, however, did not succumb. Pressing an ear to the wall, I went on listening to the darkness.

At first everything was quiet, then again I heard — far overhead — approaching footsteps. Little by little the crack in the vault began to expand. Taking hold of slippery projections in the wall, I tried to climb up it only to lose my grip and fall back down, landing on something hard: Quagga's Book of the Forgotten. Trying not to make any noise (so as not to wake Quagga), I undid its clasps and, using them as toggles, pulled myself quickly up, from one projection to the next, until my hands caught hold of the crack's widening edges. Someone's head was hanging over mine: I closed my eyes tight, threw my body outside, and rushed down the passageway without looking back. After my two wanderings in the pupil labyrinth, I more or less knew my way even in the dark. Soon I could see a light gleaming dimly from under her half-closed eyelid. I climbed out, jumped down onto the pillow and strode off, struggling against driving gusts of breath.

What if it isn't him? What if he's not mine? I thought, hovering between fear and hope. And when, finally, in the early dawn light, I began to discern my own giganticized features, when after so many days apart I saw you, my master, I vowed never again to leave you, never again to prowl about in other people's pupils. Then again, it's not I, but you who...

The little man from the pupil said no more. Tucking his black folio under his arm, he stood up. Rose-colored patches of daylight trailed across the windows. Somewhere in the distance a wheel clattered. Her eyelashes quivered. The little man glanced at them warily then turned his tired face back to me: he was awaiting my orders. "As you like it," I smiled, bringing my eyes as close as I could. He leapt up under an eyelid and strode inside me: but then something, probably a corner of the book sticking out from under his elbow, scratched the edge of my pupil and a sharp pain ricocheted through my brain. My eyes saw black. I thought it would pass, but no: the rose-colored dawn turned black; and a black night hush descended, as though time, crouched down on its paws, had slunk backwards. I slipped out of bed, quickly dressed and quietly opened the door: the corridor; a turn; a door; another door; and, feeling the wall as I went, one step then another — and out. Onto the street. I walked straight ahead, without turning, without knowing where or why. Gradually the air began to thin, freeing the outlines of the buildings. I looked back: a second dawn of bluish crimson was catching me up.

Suddenly, somewhere overhead, in a bell perch, bells, banging copper against copper, began to clang. I looked up. From the pediment of an old brick church, painted into the triangle, a gigantic eye fixed me through the mist.

Between my shoulder blades chills prickled like pinpricks: "Painted bricks." That's all it is. As I disengaged myself from the whorls of fog, I kept repeating: just painted bricks — nothing more.

Coming towards me through the light-shot mist I spied a familiar bench: here I had waited — not so very long ago — for the darkness to join me. Now the slats of the bench were mottled with glimmers and drops of dew.

I sat down on its damp edge and recalled: here the novella about the little man from the pupil, still hazy and vague, had first visited me. Now I had enough material to flesh out my theme. With the new day approaching, I began to consider how to say everything without saying anything. For a start, I must cross out the truth; no one needs that. Then variegate the pain throughout. Yes, yes. Then add a touch of the day-to-day and over all, like varnish over paint, a veneer of physiology — you can't do without that. Finally, a few philosophical bits and... Reader, you're turning away, you want to put these lines out of your sight. No, no. Don't leave me on this long empty bench: hold my hand — that's right — tight, tighter still — I've been alone for too long. I want to say to you what I've never said to anyone: why, in the end, make little children afraid of the dark when one can soothe them with it and lead them into dreams?

*1927*

# The Runaway Fingers

Two thousand ears turned towards the pianist Heinrich Dorn as he calmly adjusted the wicker seat of his swivel stool with long white fingers... Seated with his coattails hanging down, his fingers jumped up onto the piano's black case — and cantered down the straight, ivory-paved road. At first they proceeded, polished nails flashing, from a high octave C to the treble's last, glassily tinkling keys. There a black panel waited — the edge of the keyboard box: the fingers wanted to go further — they stamped distinctly and fractionally on the last two keys (eyes here and there in the hall narrowed: "what a trill!") — then spun round on their taper ends shod in fine epidermis and, leaping over one another, galloped back. Halfway along the fingers slackened their pace, musingly choosing now black, now white keys for a footfall that was soft, but deeply impressed upon the strings.

Two thousand ears leaned towards the stage.

A familiar nervous trembling seized the fingers: poised on those string-pressing hammers, they suddenly, in a single bound, hurled themselves a distance of twelve keys, coming to rest on C-Es-G-B.

Pause.

And again, cutting loose from the chord, the fingers raced away in a rapid passage to the end of the keyboard. The pianist's right hand made to pull back, to the middle register, but the rambunctious fingers refused: on they flew at breakneck speed: the fourth octave's glassy tinkles flashed past, the treble's additional keys squeaked, the keyboard frame's black shelf rapped them on the nails: tugging desperately, the fingers suddenly wrested themselves, hand and all, from under the pianist's cuff and jumped — the diamond on the little finger glinting — down onto the floor. The waxed wood of the parquet sent stabs of pain up their joints, but the fingers, without missing a beat, picked themselves up and — now mincing along on their pink shields of nails, now vaulting high into the air in a series of finger-by-finger, arpeggio-like leaps — hared towards the exit.

The huge obtuse toe of someone's boot nearly barred the way. Someone else's dirty sole briefly pinned the little finger to the carpet. Hugging the pinched pinkie to them, the fingers darted under a floor-length curtain. But a second later the curtain was twitched up to reveal two black columns that widened at the top: the fingers understood — here was the hem of a dress of one of Dorn's admirers. Swinging round on the ring finger, they sprang aside.

There wasn't a minute to lose. All about people were beginning to whisper. The whispers became murmurs, the murmurs a hubbub, the hubbub an outcry, and the outcry the roar and riot of a thousand feet.

"Catch them! Catch them!"

"What?"

"Where?!"

Part of the audience rushed up to the pianist: he was slumped on his stool in a deep faint; his left hand had flopped onto his knee, the empty cuff of his right still lay on the keyboard.

But the runaway fingers had no time for Dorn: working their long phalanges, bending and unbending their joints, they were sprinting *prestissimo* down the passageway towards the outcroppings of the stairs.

With wails and squeals, elbows elbowing elbows, people scrambled out of the way. From the hall came more cries of: "Catch them! Where? What?" But the stairs had been left behind.

In one masterly bound, the fingers sailed over the threshold and out onto the street. The riot and racket broke off. The blank benighted square, wreathed in a yellow necklace of lamplights, gaped in silence.

2

The manicured fingers of the famous pianist Heinrich Dorn, long used to strolling only along the ivory keys of concert pianos, were unaccustomed to walking along a wet and dirty pavement.

Now that they found themselves on the square's cold and sticky asphalt, picking their way through the spittle and puddles of slush, the fingers realized the folly and extravagance of their prank.

But too late. Over the threshold of the building behind, shoes, boots and walking sticks were already clattering: to return now would mean being crushed. Pressing its aching little finger to its ring finger, Dorn's right hand leaned against a scabrous curbstone and observed the scene.

The doors disgorged all the people then clapped shut — leaving the fugitive fingers alone on the empty square.

It began to drizzle. The fingers would have to find lodgings for the night. Sopping their fine white skin in puddles and gutters, they lagged, now tripping, now slipping, along the street. Suddenly, from out of the fog, a metal wheel rim came thundering past, spewing clumps of mud.

The fingers barely managed to dodge: shaking off the foul splatters in disgust, they clambered, on tremulous phalanges faint with nervous exhaustion, up onto the sidewalk and kept close to the buildings, massed in a solid phalanx.

The hour was late. A yellow clockface struck two. Shop doors were shuttered, the corrugated metal eyelids of windows lowered. Someone's belated footsteps approached and then faded away. Where to hide?

Half a keyboard up from the sidewalk bricks, the light of a swaying lantern glowed in the wind. Under the light, screwed into the wall, hung a rectangular collection box: *For the church.*

They had no choice: the fingers scrabbled up the wall's jagged edges to the cornice of the kirk, then leapt down from the cornice onto the sloping lid of the collection box. The slot in the lid was narrow, but the pianist's fingers were not famed for their fineness and agility for nothing: they squeezed through the opening and... jumped. Inside it was dark, except for a dim red spangle of light dropped in the box by the lantern.

Next to the spangle was a crumpled and obliging banknote. Chilled to the marrow, the fingers made a fist and curled up in a corner of the metal box, covered themselves with the banknote and lay still. Their stiff joints ached; their cracked and broken nails itched; the little finger was swollen and the thin band of the diamond ring cut deep into its skin.

But weariness won out: the crimson spangle of light swayed from side to side while the rain rat-tatted a familiar *moto perpetuo* on the roof of the box with springy drops. Through the slot, narrowing its emerald eyes, peered Sleep.

3

The fingers gave themselves a good shake, smoothed their swollen joints and tried to stretch out at full length on their hard bed. A crimson ray of dawn had embraced the lantern's slowly fading spangle.

The rain had abated. Having jumped up once or twice and bumped against the ceiling, the fingers wriggled gingerly through the slot and sat down on the damp slant of the collection-box roof.

An early morning wind dandled the leafless branches of the poplar trees. Below, puddles shimmered; above, clouds glowered.

As unusual as the situation was, the fingers' long-established habit of practicing for an hour and a half every morning compelled them to climb up onto the cornice of the church and run a methodical scales-like race from end to end, from right to left and from left to right, until their joints were warm and supple.

When they had finished their exercises, the fingers jumped down onto the collection box, straddled the slot and began dreaming about the recent past, now torn away...

Tucked under the warm atlas of a quilt; morning ablutions in warm soapy water; a pleasant stroll along the gently yielding keys, and then... and then the attendant fingers of the left hand dress them in a chamois leather glove, fasten the buttons, and Dorn carries them forth, cradled in the pocket of his warm coat. Suddenly the chamois is pulled off and someone's fine perfumed nails, trembling slightly, touch the fingers. They press themselves ardently to the pink nails and...

Suddenly a gnarled hand with dirty yellow nails knocked the abstracted fingers off the cant of the collection box. The hand belonged to a weak-sighted old woman on her way home from the market. Having put her basket full of parcels down on the ground, she had gone up to the collection box and felt about with a doddering hand for the slot, intending to contribute her meager mite. But just then something soft and alive grabbed her finger, jerked back and went head over heels. She heard a rustling among the paper parcels — and suddenly, five human fingers *without the human*, flicking off flour, jumped out of her basket and shot down the sidewalk.

Dropping coins, the frightened old woman crossed herself again and again and lisped a prayer with her toothless, quivering mouth.

From cobble to cobble, plunging through puddles and gutters, the fingers ran on and on.

Two small boys, squatting by a gutter and engaged in launching a toy boat with a paper sail, noticed the fingers crouching at the edge of the curb as they prepared to jump across the noisy canal. The boys' mouths fell open. Their abandoned sailboat ran aground on the cobblestones and capsized.

"Oh-ho-ho!" the boys whooped, and raced after the fingers.

Only their extraordinary pianistic facility and fluency saved them: splashing through puddles, gashing their tender epidermis on the sharp edges of stones, they ran at the speed of Beethoven's *Appassionata*, as though fingering not scabrous cobbles, but ivory keys: the greatest masters of passage-work and glissando would have been outdone and, indeed, put to shame.

Suddenly something behind them growled, and an enormous sharp-clawed paw knocked the fugitive off its five feet. Dorn's hand fell backwards; the diamond on the little finger scraped against the sidewalk; the bloody nails stuck up in the air.

The fang-filled jaws of a watchdog leered over them: mortally tired, writhing in pain, the fingers snapped at the dog's nose and, having gained a second, rushed on, pursued by barks and yelps.

4

That night the fingers had to camp first in the downspout of a drainpipe. Later, when it again began to rain, the flagging fingers were washed out of the metal pipe — and forced to wander the dark pavement in search of dry shelter.

Through a murky basement window a light was

flickering. Picking their way along the wet sash, the poor fingers tapped shyly on the pane. Nobody came.

In the pane was a hole that had been papered over: the index finger ripped the paper, and the other fingers climbed through after it. Down onto the windowsill. In the room: not a sound. On the kitchen table by the window: not a crumb. In the iron stove, slouched on squat legs and poking its long trunk into the vent, gray-red coals smoldered. On a hard plank bed, asleep in a huddled heap, were a woman and two children; attenuated faces, eyes hidden under wrinkled blue-gray lids, bodies under fusty rags.

But on the corner of a clean white pillowcase, flecked with the yellow glimmers of an oil lamp, sat, smiling slyly, Sleep: he rubbed his emerald eyes with his glassily clear webbed paws and told the poor souls his fairy tales. His words made the stains on the walls bloom with pink blossoms, while the laundry, hanging overhead, began to float along the line in a procession of snow-white clouds.

The fingers sat decorously down on the edge of the table and listened: lulled by the sound of Sleep's soft voice they recalled the rolling course of Schumann's *Fantasie-stücke*, the mysterious leaps and appeals of *Kreisleriana*.

The pocket fugitives wanted to give something to the poor souls too: the swollen little finger still glittered with Dorn's diamond ring: doubled up with pain, the fugitives dug their mutilated nails under the gold band: clink — and the ring lay on the edge of the table.

Time to go.

It was nearly morning. Sleep began bustling about: he got

down from the pillow, packed up his dreams, and was gone. The fingers followed suit: a cautious rustling of the window's torn papering — and they were again on the pavement.

A wet spring snow of white stars was falling into puddles of slush.

The fingers had no strength left: crumpled against the pavement's cold stone, they pressed thumb, index and middle finger together and fell asleep beneath the soft flights of white stars. In that same instant they suddenly heard the hardened ground begin to rock like countless piano keys; crashing against black and white, dropping drops of sun from their phalanges, coming straight for the fugitives, bearing down on them, were ruthlessly gigantic fingers.

5

A music critic came running into Dorn's study clutching a newspaper.

"Look at this!"

On page eight, circled in red pencil, was this notice:

FOUND
Five fingers
From someone's right hand
Inquire at: Dessingstrasse, 7, Apt. 54
Telephone: 3.45
Bezirk 1 — 9

Dorn dashed out into the vestibule and grabbed his coat off the hook, jamming his awkward empty cuff into the right sleeve.

"Maestro, it's too early," the critic fussed. "One inquires 'between 11 and 1' and now it's only a quarter to ten. Besides..."

But Dorn was already flying down the stairs.

Half an hour later, when the pianist Heinrich Dorn saw his runaway fingers at the bottom of a cardboard box lined with cotton wool, he began to cry: the fingers, still pressed together, lay motionless in a hideous lump, their cracked and ulcerated skin caked with mud. Their once fine tips, now repulsively flattened, bore the yellow excrescences of calluses; the nails were broken and lacerated; dried blood was turning black under the bends of the joints.

"They're dead," whispered a white-lipped Dorn, reaching with the clumsy empty funnel of his cuff for the motionless fingers. Just then the little finger twitched: but barely.

Dorn, his teeth frantically chattering, edged his right arm towards the box: the fingers, tossing about and becoming entangled in the whorls of cotton wool, raised themselves up uncertainly on their tremulous phalanges and suddenly, all aflutter, jumped inside the cuff.

Dorn laughed and cried at the same time: on his knees, sticking out of crisp white cuffs, lay two hands: one with white, tapering, manicured fingers smelling of expensive cologne, the other a brownish gray color, calloused and covered with rough, abraded skin.


Two weeks later Heinrich Dorn returned to the stage with the first in a celebrated series of concerts.

The pianist played differently somehow: gone were the

dazzling passages, the lightening glissandos and emphatic grace notes. The pianist's fingers seemed loath to amble down that short, seven-octave road paved with ivory keys. Then again there were moments when it seemed as though someone's gigantic fingers — torn away from another keyboard, extended from another world — dropping drops of sun from their phalanges, were skipping along the piano's skimpy, squeaky and rickety keys: and then thousands of ears leaned forward — on necks craned towards the stage.

But that was only at moments.

Connoisseurs, one after another — on tiptoe — walked out of the hall.

*1922*

# Autobiography of a Corpse

Journalist Shtamm, whose "Letters from the Provinces" were signed *Etal*, among other pseudonyms, had decided to set out — on the heels of his letters — for Moscow.

Shtamm believed in his elbows and in the ability of Etal to swap drops of ink for rubles, but the matter of living space disturbed him. He knew that on the metropolitan chessboard, squares had not been set aside for all of the chessmen. People who had been to Moscow scared you: the buildings are all packed to the rafters. You have to camp: in vestibules, on backstairs, boulevard benches, in asphalt cauldrons and dustbins.

That is why Shtamm, as soon as he stepped off the train onto the Moscow station platform, began repeating into dead and living, human and telephonic ears one and the same word: *a room...*

But the black telephonic ear, having heard him out, hung indifferently on its steel hook. And the human ears hid from him under fur and astrakhan collars — the frost that day crackled underfoot — while the word, as though landing under more and more layers of carbon paper, grew fainter with each repetition and broke up into softly knocking letters.

Citizen Shtamm was a very nervous and impressionable person: that evening when, spun out like a top on a string, he lay down on three hard chairs determined to push him to the floor with their backs, he saw the specter of the dustbin, its wooden lid thrown hospitably open, in his mind's eye.

But there's truth in the old adage: morning is wiser than evening. Wilier, too, no doubt. Having risen with the dawn from his chairs, which went straight back to their corners to sulk, Shtamm apologized for the trouble, thanked them for the bed and trudged off along the half-deserted streets of snow- and rime-clad Moscow. But before he had gone a hundred paces, at practically the first crossroads, he met a little man mincing along in a thin and threadbare overcoat. The little man's eyes were hidden beneath a cap, his lips tightly muffled in a scarf. In spite of this, the man saw him, stopped and said:

"Oh. And you too?"

"Yes."

"Where so early?"

"I'm looking for a room."

Shtamm did not catch the man's reply: the words stuck fast in the scarf's double whorls. But he saw him thrust a hand inside his overcoat, feel about for something and finally pull out a narrow notebook. He quickly wrote something in it, blowing on his frozen fingers. An hour later, a three-by-four-inch slip of paper torn out of the notebook had miraculously turned into a living space measuring one hundred square feet.

The longed-for space had been found on the top floor of an enormous gray building in one of the by-streets that trace crooked zigzags between Povarskaya and Nikitskaya. The room struck Shtamm as somewhat narrow and dark, but once the electric light had been switched on, gay blue roses appeared, tripping down the wallpaper in long verticals. Shtamm liked the blue roses. He went to the window: hundreds upon hundreds of roofs pulled low over windows. Looking pleased, he turned round to the proprietress — a quiet, elderly woman with a black shawl over her shoulders:

"Very good. I'll take it. May I have the key?"

There was no key. The proprietress looked down and, pulling her shawl about her with a shiver, said the key had been lost, but that... Shtamm wasn't listening:

"Doesn't matter. For now a padlock will do. I'll go and fetch my things."

In another hour the new lodger was tinkering with the door, screwing in the padlock's iron hasp. Elated as Shtamm was, one small detail did bother him: while securing the temporary bolt, he noticed that the old lock seemed to have been broken. Above the iron lock body he descried the marks of blows and deep scratches. A little higher up, on the wooden stock, he found the manifest marks of an axe. Feeling not a little apprehensive, Shtamm lighted a match (the corridor connecting his room to the entrance hall was dark) and made a thorough inspection of the door. But nothing else — save the legible white number 24, inscribed in the middle of the door's flat brown surface and, evidently, necessary for the house accounts — did he notice.

"Doesn't matter," Shtamm waved the thought away and set about unpacking his suitcase.

The next two days everything went as it was supposed to go. From morning till night Shtamm went from door to door, from meeting to meeting, bowing, shaking hands, talking, listening, asking, demanding. Come evening, the briefcase under his elbow now strangely heavy and weighing his arm down, his steps shorter, slower and less steady, Shtamm would return to his room, look blearily round at the ranks of blue wallpaper roses and sink into a black, dreamless sleep. The third evening he managed to finish somewhat earlier. The minute hand on the street-clock face jerked forward to show 10:45 as Shtamm approached the entrance to his building. He climbed the stairs and, trying not to make any noise, turned the cam of the American lock on the outer door. Then he went down the unlighted corridor to room No. 24 and stopped, fumbling in his pocket for the key. The other rooms were dark and quiet. Except for the hum — to the left, through three thin walls — of a primus-stove. He found the key, turned it inside the steel body and gave the door a shove: in that same instant a white blur by his fingers rustled, slipped down and flopped on the floor. Shtamm snapped on the light. By the threshold, having evidently fallen out of the crack in the door, lay a white paper packet. Shtamm picked it up and read the address:

*Resident*

*Room No. 24*

There was no name. Shtamm folded back a corner of the copybook inside: angular jumping letters bunched in a nervous line looked up. Puzzled, Shtamm again read the strange address, but in that instant, as he was turning the manuscript over, it slipped out of its capacious paper noose and smoothed out its folded-in-four body by itself. After that Shtamm had only to turn to the first page, which bore only these words: *Autobiography of a Corpse.*

No matter who you, the person in room 24, are — the manuscript began — you are the only person I shall ever make happy: you see, had I not vacated my hundred sq. feet by hanging myself from the hook in the left-hand corner by the door of your current quarters, you would hardly have found yourself a resting place with such ease. I write about this in the past tense: an exactly calculated future may be thought of as a *fait accompli*, that is to say, almost as the past.

We are not acquainted and now it seems too late for us ever to be so, but that in no way prevents my knowing you: you are from the provinces. *Such* rooms, you see, are better rented to out-of-towners with no knowledge of local affairs and press reports. Naturally, you have come to "conquer Moscow"; you have the requisite energy and desire "to gain a foothold", "to make your way in the world". In short, you have that particular ability I never had: the ability to be alive.

Well, I am certainly ready to cede my square feet to you. Or rather: I, a corpse, agree to move over a little. Go on and live: the room is dry, the neighbors quiet and peaceful, and there's a view. True, the wallpaper was tattered and stained, but *for you* I had it replaced: and here I think I managed to guess your taste: blue roses flattened in silly verticals: people like you like that sort of thing. Isn't that so?

In exchange for the solicitude and consideration I have shown you, the person in room No. 24, I ask only for a simple reader's consideration of this manuscript. I do not need you, my successor and confessor, to be wise and subtle: no, I need from you only one very rare quality: that you be *completely alive*.

For more than a month now I have been tortured by insomnias. Over the next three nights they will help me to tell you what I've never told anyone. After that, a neatly soaped noose may be applied as a radical cure for insomnia.

An old Indian folktale tells of a man made to shoulder a corpse night after night — till the corpse, its dead but moving lips pressed to his ear, has finished telling the story of its long-over life. Do not try to throw me to the ground. Like the man in the folktale, you will have to shoulder the burden of my three insomnias and listen patiently, till the corpse has finished its autobiography.

Having read up to this line, Shtamm again examined the broad paper label-band: it bore no stamps, no postmark.

"I can't understand it," he muttered, walking to the door and standing there plunged in thought. The hum of the primus had long since quieted. Through the walls: not a sound. Shtamm glanced over at the copybook: it lay open on the table, waiting. He delayed a minute, then went obediently back, sat down and found the lost line with his eyes:

I have worn lenses over my pupils for a long time. Every year I have to increase their strength: my vision is now 8.5. That means that 55% of the sunlight does not exist for me. I have only to press my biconcave ovals back into their case — and space, as though it too had been shut up in that dark and cramped compartment, suddenly contracts and fogs. I see only gray blurs, murk and long threads of transparent dots. Sometimes, when I wipe my slightly dusty lenses with a piece of chamois, I have an odd feeling: what if along with the specks of dust that have settled on their glassy concavities I should wipe away all of *space*? Now you see it — now you don't: like a sheen.

I am always acutely aware of this glassy adjunct that has stolen up to my eyes on bent wiry legs. One day I realized that it could break more than the rays of light falling inside its ovals. The absurdity I am about to describe occurred some years ago: several chance meetings with a girl I half knew had created a strange bond between us. I remember she was young, her face a delicate oval. We were reading the same books, and so we used similar words. After our first meeting I noticed that her myopically dilated pupils in fine blue rims, hidden (like mine) behind the lenses of a pince-nez, were affectionately, but relentlessly following me. One day we were left alone together; I touched her hands; they responded with a light pressure. Our lips moved closer together — and at that very moment the absurdity happened: in my clumsiness I jostled her lenses with mine: caught in a wiry embrace, they slipped off and landed on the carpet with a high, thin tinkle. I bent down to pick them up. In my hands I held two strange glass creatures, their crooked metal legs so entangled as to create one hideous four-eyed creature. Quivering specks of light, jumping from lens to lens, vibrated voluptuously inside the ovals. I pulled them apart: with a thin tinkle, the coupling lenses came unhooked.

There was a knock at the door.

I glimpsed the girl trying, with trembling fingers, to press the recalcitrant lentils back into place, against her eyes.

A minute later I was on my way down the stairs. I felt as though I had tripped over a corpse in the dark.

I left. Forever. In vain did she try to catch me up with a letter: its jumping lines begged me to forget something and promised with a naive simplicity to "always remember". Yes, remembering me always in my new corpselike condition could stand me in good stead, but... as I searched her note, letter by letter, I felt that the glassily transparent cold within me would not lessen.

With particular care I examined my name: on the envelope. Yes, nine letters: and they were calling me. I heard them. But I would not answer.

It was then, I remember, that the period of dead, empty days began. They had come before. And gone. But now I knew: they had come for good. .

This didn't cause me any pain, or even uneasiness. Only boredom. Or rather: boredoms. A late 18th-century book I once read called them "Earthly Boredoms". Exactly. There are many boredoms: there is Spring boredom when identical people love other identical people, when the ground is covered with puddles, the trees with green pustules. And a series of tedious Autumn boredoms when the sky sheds stars, clouds shed rain, trees shed leaves, and the "I" sheds its own self.

At the time I was living not in your, forgive me, *our* room 24, but in an unnumbered roomlet in a small five-window annex in the provinces. The panes were spattered with rain. But even through the spatters I could see the trees in the garden swaying rhythmically in time to the wind's blows like people tormented by toothache. I ordinarily sat in a splayed armchair, among my books and boredoms. The boredoms were many: I had only to close my eyes — and I could hear them sliding across the creaky floorboards, lazily dragging their felt-shod feet.

For days on end, from dusk to dusk, I thought of myself as a *biconcave creature*, impossible to reach *outwardly or inwardly*, from without or from within: both were equally forbidden. Beyond reach.

Sometimes I too, like a tree tormented by the wind, would sway rhythmically between the oak arms of my armchair, in time to the tedious swaying of an idea: the dead, the idea loomed, are to be envied. Barely stiff, and down goes the lid; on top of the lid goes damp earth; and on top of the damp earth, sod. And that's that. But here, just begin bumping along in a dray, and they will cart you on and on like that, from pothole to pothole, through spring and winter, from one decade to the next, unmourned and unneeded.

Now, when I think back on my state then, I cannot understand how a trifle to do with some pieces of glass could have so wounded and disconcerted me. It's not clear to me how my soul, if I still had one then, could have been crushed and desoulerated by such a speck of dust. But at the time, I took that trifle as an object lesson given me by my "glassy adjunct". As it was, my attempts to penetrate the world beyond my biconcave ovals had been few and fearful. If the formula *natura abhorret vacuum*\* has been disproved, now I know why its inversion — *vacuum abhorret naturam*\*\* — has yet to come under attack. I think it will prevail.

At any rate, I ceased all attempts to enter my *outer* self. All those passes at friendship, experiments with another person's "I", efforts to give or take love — I must, thought I, forget and renounce them once and for all. For some time I had been mentally constructing a *flattened little world* in which *everything* would be in *here* — a little world that one could lock shut inside one's room.

"Space," I reasoned while still in earliest youth, "is absurdly vast and has expanded — with its orbits, stars and yawning parabolas — to infinity. But if one absorbs it into numbers and meanings, it can easily fit on two or three bookshelves. I have long preferred the narrow margins of books to the monotonous miles of fields on this earth; the spine of a book has always seemed more intelligent to me than confused sermons about "the roots of things"; the sheer accumulation of those things, everywhere one looks, seems crude and meaningless compared to the wise and subtle

---

\* Nature abhors a vacuum (*Lat.*).

\*\* A vacuum abhors nature (*Lat.*).

concantenations of letters and symbols hidden away in books. Though the lines in books have deprived me of half of my eyesight (55%), I do not resent them: they knew too well how to be meek and dead. Only they, those silent black signs, could deliver me, however briefly, from the power of my burdensome, listless and sleepy boredoms. It was then, while finishing at the Institute of Oriental Studies, that I lost myself in the painstaking work of my dissertation: *The Letter "T" in Turkic Languages.*

I still feel deeply indebted to that little two-handled "T" for the pains it took and the help it gave me during that black lightless time. "T" led my eyes from lexicon to lexicon, down long columns of words, and so kept me from sinking even for a second into oblivion; that tiny, black-bodied letter stirred up the dust on my books, showed me tangled paragraphs in old glossaries and collections of syntagms. Sometimes, in an effort to amuse me, it played hide-and-go-seek: I would hunt for that tiny sign, twirling my pencil along the lines and down the margins of a book, until I found it hidden in among other letters and symbols. Sometimes I even smiled at this. Yes, I smiled. But the companion of my leisure could be of greater comfort still. "You see, 'I' is just a letter," "T" would say, "just as I am. That's all it is. Is it really worth grieving over? Now you see it — now you don't."

I remember that then, in between other things, as a diversion, I began studying the *philology* of "I". My notes — if only they aren't lost — must still be in a folder somewhere. But I haven't time to look for them now. I quote from memory (inaccurately, I'm afraid): "'I' has a changeable

root, but always a short phoneme. I-ich-moi-я-yo-εγω-io-
ego-аз. One can hypothesize the process of its shortening,
or 'contraction'. Most likely it is the result of ordinary speech
patterns. Phonetically, however, much remains unclear.
Incidentally, a count of the word 'ich' in Stirner showed that
nearly 25% of the text consists of 'ich' (if you count all its
derivatives). Keep that up, and the whole text will soon be
one continuous 'I'. Yet if one searches life: is there much 'I'
in it?"

Come dusk the bustling "T" would go exhausted to bed,
usually under a bookmark, while I, not wishing to bother it
anymore, would pace from corner to corner in the dark.
And every time I clearly heard my soul — with a high thin
tinkle, drop by drop — dissolving into the emptiness. The
drops were rhythmic and resounding, they had that same
familiar glassy ring. This may have been a pseudo-
hallucination, I don't know: it doesn't matter to me. But at
the time I gave this phenomenon a special name: *psychorrhea*.
Meaning "soul seepage".

Sometimes that rhythmic flight — drop by drop — into
emptiness even frightened me. I would turn on the light and
shoo both the dusk and the pseudo-sound away. The dusk,
the boredoms, the hallucinations, and "T" would all disappear:
it was then that that ultimate loneliness, known to but a few
of the living, began, when you are left not only without others,
but *without yourself*.

There was, however, a sort of *other person*, a foreign
*something*, which disturbed my black leisure. From a fairly
young age, you see, I was visited by a strange *figment*: 0.6

person. This figment arose as follows: one day I was rummaging in a geography textbook when I came across this line: "In the country's northern latitudes the population per square mile is 0.6 person." It stuck in my mind's eye like a splinter. I squinted and saw: a flat white field stretching to the horizon and beyond, a field divided into right-angled square miles. Snow falling in listless, lazy flakes. And in every square at the intersection of diagonals, *it*: round-shouldered, spindly and bent low to the bare, ice-covered ground: *0.6 person*. Exactly: 0.6. Not just half, not half a person. Here a fractional, dissymmetricizing fillip had latched on to "just". The *incompleteness* — contradictory as this may seem — had been infiltrated by a *remainder*, an "over and above".

I tried to banish the image. But it stuck. Then suddenly, one of those half-creatures (I could clearly see the ones in the squares closest to my eyes) slowly began to turn towards me. I wanted to avert my eyes, but I couldn't: it was as if they had fused with the dead empty eye sockets of 0.6.

And there was not a blade of grass anywhere, not so much as an ice-covered rock, not a speck; only windless air and listless, loosely falling snowflakes.

Thereafter, 0.6 person took to coming to see me on my empty days. During my black intervals. This was no apparition, vision, or sleepy reverie. No, it was just that: a figment.

Now, when I try to describe as exactly as possible the accident, shall we say, that befell my "I", as described above, I am helped by symbols of mathematical logic. A point in space may be found, they say, only by means of intersecting coordinates. But if those coordinates come apart then... space is vast, while a point has no size at all. Evidently, my coordinates had come apart, and to find me, a psychic point in infinity, turned out to be impossible.

Or clearer still: the study of curves includes certain imaginary lines which, when they cross, produce a real *point*. True, the "reality" of this point is of a peculiar sort: out of fiction. Perhaps that will be *my* case too.

Be that as it may, I did not inform "friends" and "acquaintances." I did not beg for the expressions of "regret" due me. I did not bother about a small black frame for my name. I thought only of how to incorporate that imaginary "psychic point" more firmly and reliably into the compact square of my living space, out of sight of all those bad mathematicians incapable of distinguishing the real from the imaginary, the dead from the living. Relations, acquaintances, and even friends have an exceedingly poor grasp of non-obviousnesses; until a person is served up to them in a coffin as a *cadaver vulgaris*\* under a trihedral lid, with two five-kopeck coins over the eyes, they will keep cornering that person with their dogged condolences, questions and "how do you dos".

After finishing my studies, I moved to Moscow and enrolled in the University's department of pure mathematics. I never finished. One day, having left the library with a four-volume dictionary of philosophy (Gogotsky's) under my arm,

---

\* Ordinary corpse (*Lat.*).

I was walking down a long, vaulted corridor when my path was blocked by a crowd of students jamming the doors to the auditorium. Obviously a strike. I could see someone's head sticking up out of the crowd, screaming in a strange bird-like voice, and craning a blue-collared neck:

"Anyone who doesn't belong here should leave. Everyone else into the auditorium."

I had meant to go home but the words "doesn't belong" hobbled my legs. Clutching my dictionary volumes, which had begun to slip in the crush, I stepped into the lecture hall. The doors closed. First came long, obscure speeches. Then a short word: police. The heavy lexicon suddenly began to weigh my arms down unbearably. They took our names and escorted us — between bayonets — to the Manège. Another door closed. I felt more and more baffled. The excitement all round me had clearly subsided. Some faces looked almost abject.

I was bored. The minutes crawled by on the wall clock. The double doors would not open. I began leafing through my dictionary. It was a sort of bibliographical curiosity. One of the first 19th-century editions. My eye was immediately caught by the word *Ethics*.

Then I understood: this old dictionary was an intelligent conversationalist. Well, of course: only old-fashioned and inarticulate Ethics could have shut me up inside a manège with all these people for whom I had no use.

Now, on reviewing my memories, I see that my thinking was invariably flawed by a fatal miscalculation, a mistake, which I stubbornly persisted in making: I considered everything that took place under my frontal bone to be unique. I had imagined *psychorrhea* in only *one specimen*. I never suspected that the process of mental deadening could be creeping — from skull to skull, from an individual to a group, from a group to a class, from a class to an entire social organism. Hiding my half-existence behind the opaque walls of my skull, concealing it like a shameful disease, I did not consider the simple fact that the same thing could be occurring under other skullcaps, in other locked rooms.

The other day, while leafing through *Rerum Moscoviticarum Commentarii* by Herberstein, who visited Russia in the early 16th century, I found this sentence: "Some of them derive the name of their country from the Aramaic word Ressaia or Resessaia which means: a spray of drops."

If those "some" existed so long ago, then, multiplying from one century to the next, they must gradually have seized hold of all the levers and signaling devices of that "life". They saw Russia — and forced Russia to be seen — as Ressaia: a spray of isolated drops. Over long decades of work that stultified life, they perfected and refined their technique of splintering society until they had either destroyed or numbed the connective tissue knitting its cells into one. We lived like separated drops. Like waifs. A university regulation in '93 tried to break us up into "auditors". As early as a century ago, Chelyshev noted the emergence of products of mental disintegration: he wrote about "the hermits in their studies". It is we, the last-born generation, who evolved the philosophical principle about another person's "I": the "I" that is not mine is foreign and alien, irreducible to *you*. People-droplets know neither channels, nor currents. For them, "I" and "we" are separated by gulfs. Gulfs are what successive generations of social waifs have fallen into. They need only be buried. And forgotten.

Now I understand: the "I" that is not nourished by "we", not umbilically connected to the maternal organism enveloping its small life, cannot begin to be itself. The mollusk too, hidden inside its tight-shut valves, if one *helps* those valves by binding them with a tight metal band, will die.

But at the time we weren't able to grasp this thought in its entirety because our very thinking was deformed: the routes of our logics had been severed.

The thought thought either no further than "I", or no closer than the "cosmos". On reaching the "threshold of one's consciousness", the line between "I" and "we", it would stop and either turn back or take a monstrous leap into "starriness" — the transcendent — "other worlds".

Sight had either a *microscopic* or a *telescopic* radius: whatever was too far for the microscope or too close for the telescope was simply *lost from sight*, and not included in any way by anyone in the field of vision.

It's nearly dawn. I'm tired. I must stop for now. All round me, both through the walls and outside, it is somehow especially quiet and still. My insomnias have taught me to sense the night's movements and minutes. Long ago I noticed that just before dawn, when a dark blue glimmer clings to the window and the stars grow blind, there is a particularly profound hush. As there is now: through the frozen panes I can see, but dimly (I've put out the light): in the blue gloom the dark steep slants of roofs: exactly like the upturned hulls of sunken ships. And beneath them rows of black mute holes. Further down are the bare ice-covered branches of stunted city trees. Empty streets. And windless air steeped in numbness and silence. This is *my hour*: at this hour I shall probably...

The text broke off in mid-sentence. The next seven lines had been carefully crossed out. Shtamm skipped over the inky parallels and went on reading. Through the wall a clock struck four.

## The second night

All that playing at peacemaking might have gone on and on had the cannons not started to pound. At first the cannons hit somewhere far way, hit other people. Then they began pounding close at hand, pounding our people. And when the cannons had finished pounding, the stamping devices started to pound. The work of muzzles on bodies left round black craters. The stamps did not hit people: only their names. But even so: their names, like those broken bodies, were blotched with blue and black circles.

Chance threw me up on a southern bridgehead. The city in which I lived changed hands thirteen times. Regimes came. And went. And returned. And left again. And with every regime came: cannons and stamping devices.

That's when it happened: on the eve of yet another regime change, as I was sifting through a heap of old and new "identity cards", I discovered something missing: my identity.

Of the cards there were quantities. But my identity had vanished. Not a copy anywhere. I must have overlooked it: that was my first thought.

But after going all through that stamporated junk a second time, paper by paper, I still could not find my "identity". I had expected this: the more they *made certain of my identity*, the less certain I became of it myself: my old half-forgotten illness, psychorrhea, jogged by the blows of the stamping devices, was returning. The more often the disjunctional Remington lines *assured* me with a No., ornate signatures and a seal that I really was so-and-so, the more suspicious I became of my "reality", the more keenly I felt that I was both *this* person and *that*. Little by little I developed a passion: I wanted more and more stamporated forms, and no matter how many I amassed, I still felt uncertain. The nearly staunched process had recommenced: the caverns in my "I" had again begun to expand. With each new stamp *my sense of myself* grew weaker: I — and I — half-I — barely-I — slightly-I: it was melting away.

The feeling my then *I* had poring over that pile of my stamporated names was not one of despair or grief. It was rather a sort of bitter joy. "Here lies," I thought, "my cold and dead name. It was alive. But now, just look, it's riddled with cadaverous blue stamps. So be it."

As you, the person in room 24, can see, your predecessor has nothing against a good joke. Even the thought of my present manipulations with hook and noose cannot keep me from smiling. Yes, I am smiling and, who knows, perhaps not for the last time. But this is only a diagram: from — to.

The material about the war, of course, requires a more detailed and serious exposition. So I'll begin:

One July night in 1914 I was working on an article about "The Axiomatism Crisis" when I suddenly heard carts clattering outside. Our side-street, as you'll soon see, is quiet and deserted. The sound bothered me: I put my manuscript aside, preferring to wait out the noise. But it didn't stop. A train of empty wagons, wheels banging against the cobbles, was rattling past down below and preventing the silence from closing in. My nerves were slightly ajangle from writing. I didn't want to sleep. But since my work had come to a halt, I put my coat on and went out. The nighttime zigzags of our back streets seemed strangely animated. Excited people were bunched together on corners all talking at once. Over and again, I heard the word "war".

Glinting here and there on the walls of buildings I saw paper squares. Only yesterday afternoon they hadn't been there.

I walked up to one. The shadow from a cornice cut off the top lines. I began reading from somewhere in the middle:

> *"...are being bought up by the commissariat:*
> *foot wrappings — 7 kop.; undershirt — 26 kop.;*
> *boots (mil. type) — 6 rub. per pair, also..."*

Only by holding a lighted match up to the paper square's top lines did I realize that it was collecting not only boots and undershirts, but bodies with what was in them: life. About the price of this last item, it said nothing.

By morning multicolored flags were hanging over building entrances and gateways. Men with newspapers held up to their eyes were walking along the sidewalks; other men with rifles slung over their shoulders were walking along the roadways. Thus from the very first day, newspapers and rifles divided us all: into *those* who were to die, and *those* for whom they were to die.

At the outset, of course, there was much confusion and chaos. A group of people would crowd round some gawky new recruit in his long greatcoat the color of earth and sputter joyfully:

"Are you for us?"

"We're for you."

But later the nebulous line dividing "those who" from "those for whom" became more distinct, and along that line there now ran a crack; the crack's edges opened and began to widen.

Whatever it was, the early days of the war excited even me somewhat. I had operated too much and too often with the "death" symbol, had included that *biological minus* in my formulas too systematically, not to be affected in some way by all that was taking place around me. Death — a dissociation that I imagined within the confines of my "I", and only my "I" (beyond was of virtually no interest to me) — was now forcing me to think in broader and more generalized terms. All the printers' ink was now going to death's accounts; death was turning into a government-recommended idea. Officially regulated, death began putting out its own periodical, which, like any well-organized publishing concern, appeared on schedule. It was the most succinct, businesslike and absorbing publication I had ever read: I am speaking of those white booklets, like fortnightlies, that provided a "complete list of the dead, wounded, and missing in action". At first glance, a death journal might seem dull: number — name — number — another name. But given a certain imagination, the dry, lapidary style of those booklets only intensified one's sense of the fantastic. They pushed one to the most surprising conclusions: having conducted a purely statistical investigation of the March and April issues for 1915, I, for instance, knew that 35% more Sidorovs had been killed than Petrovs. But then Petrovs went missing more often. Sidorovs were evidently unlucky. Or perhaps Petrovs were cowards, or else kept to the rear. I don't know. I only know that the distant, battle-scorched fields and crater-pocked earth were exerting a stronger and stronger pull on my imagination. I was *here*, among those *for whom* men were dying. They were dying far away, hundreds of miles away, so as not to disturb us. And their corpses, if they returned at all *from there to here*, returned in secret, at night, so as not to alarm us: those for whom one must die.

I remember I even gave up on my "Axiomatism Crisis". Work on it had not been going well. And some nights, I would quietly dress and slip out into the benighted streets. I knew the exact hours the ambulance trams fetched up at the lazarettos with fresh batches — just arrived from that mysterious "there" — of hashed human flesh.

As a rule, I didn't have to wait long. From around a bend in the street, steel grinding dully against steel, black, unlighted cars would come trundling out. They would pull up at the entrance. A light would flash in the doorway. The doors would swing quietly open and, while whispering orderlies tramped up and down the steps with stretchers, I would approach the half-lowered panels of the summer ambulance trams and listen to the muffled, almost soundless squirms and moans of dying human flesh. By the time the cars had been cleaned out, a new load would be creeping up from behind along the rails.

I found it hard to only look. Being *here* but drawn *there*, I couldn't do that anymore. One night, I seized the moment when several orderlies, while unloading carcasses sprawled between long poles, converged in the doorway creating a jam: I walked up to a stretcher that had been abandoned in the middle of the pavement. So as not to waste the free minute, the carriers had gone off to get a light from someone's cigarette. Now the carcass, entirely covered by a brown-gray greatcoat, was unguarded. I quickly bent down and lifted the broadcloth. I could barely see anything. Before my suddenly fogged spectacles was only a blurry smudge, writhing and twitching. A smell of sanies and sweat singed my nostrils. I bent down even lower, right to the ear of what was lying under the broadcloth:

"For us? For me? But, you see, I may *not* exist. That's just it, I don't. So it turns out that..."

I must have hurt him when I tugged at the edge of his greatcoat. Because suddenly from in there, from the twitching spot, came a soft and strained: eeeee. I unclenched my fingers: the broadcloth fell — and covered the smudge.

I hurried home, as though in a rush to get somewhere.

Yet when I got to my door, I hung back for a long time, afraid to cross the threshold. I knew that there, in that dark box of a room, patiently waiting among the symbols and numbers, was my figment: 0.6 person.

All night it tormented me with the relentless emptiness of its eye sockets.

Meanwhile, the white and pink squares pasted to the walls of buildings had been replaced by blue paper rectangles. The listed years, rising up the scale, were coming closer and closer to my "call-up year". The distant *there*, glowing blue from the paper leaves, was calling to me ever more loudly and tenderly: Come.

And it seemed to me that I heard it, that short simple syllable.

But then one day, at an intersection, I met a doctor I knew. As we were saying goodbye, I retained his hand.

"Tell me..."

"What?"

"With six diopters, do they take you?"

"Y-yes. Although..."

"What about seven?"

"No."

We unlinked hands. When he had gone a dozen paces, the doctor glanced back at me and seemed about to turn round. But he went on. At the time I had 7½. My glass adjunct was stubbornly clinging to *here*. Still standing where the doctor had left me, I unclasped its tight metal legs, held it up to my face, and studied its enormous oval-squinting double-concave eyes. It may have been a simple solar reflex or something else — I don't know — but in the eyes of my adjunct there sparkled a bright and joyful radiance.

It was then that my excruciating insomnias began. I gave up my late-night strolls about the streets. They no longer helped. And I've never been a drinker. People's society is worse for me than insomnia. But I had to fill those long empty vigils with something. I bought 32 black and white carved wooden pieces and began playing chess at night: myself against myself. The utter futility of chess thinking appealed to me. After long struggles between thoughts and counter-thoughts, pitched battles between moves and counter-moves, I could pour that tiny world, wooden and dead, back into its box, and not a trace of the dynasties of black and white kings — or the devastating wars they waged — remained: neither within me, nor without.

Still, my game of "myself against myself" did have one peculiarity that at first intrigued me: *black* almost always won.

Meanwhile long caterpillars of trains had taken away almost all the men with rifles. And left behind creatures with hands fit only for newspapers: those nervously crumpled papers, studded with numbers, either threatening or falsely promising, changed their tune from one day to the next. A purely psychological statistic doesn't (yet) exist. But, generally speaking, the war's dialectic forced all those who were more or less *alive* to go to their death; and gave all those who were more or less *dead* the right to live. And if this dialectic could only separate them, the living from the dead, then the new regime, arriving in its wake, must sooner or later pit them against each other: as enemies.

Even then one sensed the approach of this new, as yet unnamed regime. It was as though the oxygen were being pumped out of the air in bursts by a slow and gigantic plunger. The atmosphere was suffocating. Men *from here* could not and would not hide their dislike of men *from there*, the lone ones who, having snatched a two-week leave from death, tried in vain to find distraction among the unsympathetic men for whom they were fighting.

One day, when I was dusting my bookshelves, a fat German tome slipped out of my hand and landed on the floor with a soft plop. A random line in that open book caught my eye, and I read on. In the language of inhabitants of the Fiji Islands, it turned out, there is no word for "I". Savages do without that symbol we so value by replacing it with something like our "to me".

I considered that I had made an important practical discovery. Now, if I were to fall out with my "I", I might try *living in the dative case.*

To me: some bread

a female

some quiet

and a little peace Heaven. If there is any.

And perhaps...

But the events then bearing down upon us at such a catastrophic rate rendered my venture with "to me" somewhat belated.

The situation was becoming more and more alarming.

The front lines were stealing up on us. People imagined they heard distant cannonades that didn't exist. When small, tattered clouds drifted over the city, they said they came *from there*. Then launched into lengthy explanations of how gunfire alters the shapes of clouds. It was as though we, the ones still here, had been installed in an enormous thick-walled building girded round by rows of blind "false windows".

On my desk at the moment is an amusing toy for reflection. It was given to me by an engineer I knew who worked in a vacuum laboratory: an ordinary, hermetically sealed, blown-glass ball. Inside it is a meticulously twined and exceedingly fine strand of silver hair. And surrounding the strand is a vacuum, a carefully filtered void. This, to me, is the whole point of a glass ball.

The engineer explained to me that this total evacuation, this absolute void, took a long time to achieve. For only recently have we mastered the technique of making an *absolute* emptiness, a so-called *hard vacuum*.

Now the moment was approaching when I, having hidden a thought inside my fragile glass ball, would enter that hard vacuum.

I fidgeted with my gift then asked:

"But *how* do you put the air back in?"

The engineer looked at me as one does at an eccentric or a child, and burst out laughing:

"Very simple: break the glass."


**The third and last night**

I'm falling behind in my writing. I doubt I'll manage to finish by morning. The silliest thing cut into my work: sleep. And disrupted the routine of my insomnias.

Late this afternoon I suddenly couldn't keep my eyes open, and I had this dream:

I dreamt that I was here in this same cage of flat blue roses. Sitting and waiting for something. Then suddenly I heard the soft sound of wheels on snow. Strange, I thought, wheels in winter. I went to the window. A hearse was at the entrance — black with white tassels. Two or three men in dress kaftans over knitted vests were staring up at my window. No mistake there. One even shielded his eyes with his hand. I stepped back from the window, then again crept towards it, keeping to one side so they wouldn't see me: they were still staring. One man adjusted an absurd hat resembling an overturned boat, sat down on a curbstone, and lighted a cigarette. So they had decided to wait. Trying to make myself invisible, I hugged the wall and inched towards the threshold. Stepping out into the corridor, I heard the tramp of heavy boots by the front door, as though three or four men were shouldering something long and unwieldy. The door was wide open. But the doorway was narrow and the thing, dark blue with white trim and swaying on the men's shoulders, had gotten stuck. I stepped back inside, closed the door, and looked round for the key. There was no key. Meanwhile that dark blue unwieldiness with white piping, banging into walls and corners in the corridor, was coming closer and closer. I leaned my shoulder against the door and braced an outstretched foot against a leg of the bed. For good measure. And then... I woke up. My shoulder was twisted uncomfortably against the wall's blue roses. My outstretched foot was wedged into the bed's wooden back.

Still barely awake, I thought to myself: am I really afraid? And have I thought everything through? What if...

No. Whatif will no longer fool me. How well I know him, that universal marplot and jester. It is he, calling himself a Grand Peut-Etre*, who outjested that jester Rabelais by inviting him "for after death". And Rabelais believed him.

Whatif himself doesn't believe in anything: not even corpses. If he sees the lid coming down on a coffin flanked by men waiting with shovels, he'll quick slip his finger in between coffin and lid. And keep it there till it's pinched. He only gets in the way.

The censers may already be wafting incense, and the clergy singing of the last kiss; a girl brings her trembling lips to the dead, tightly pursed crack, but Whatif is right there, whispering into a waxen ear: "Don't lose your chance, comrade Deceased." Even so, I'm grateful to the marplot. He made me a gift of one day. Only one. I promised myself to remember him at the end: and so I am.

The Revolution crashed down like lightening. One can hide that lightening, its discharge, in a dynamo, and force it, fragmented and calculated on electricity meters, to flicker dimly inside the bell-jars of thousands and thousands of economic light bulbs. But then, when the Revolution was still new, we were all, willy-nilly, electrified or burned by its all-consuming bent. In an instant, all thresholds had been

---

* Great Perhaps (*Fr.*)

removed — not only from rooms, cells, and studies, but also from consciousnesses. Words one had thought forever crushed by the censors' pencils, shrunk and shunted into breviers and nonpareils, suddenly revived and began fluttering and calling from red flags and banners. And having suddenly overcome my threshold, I too crept out to meet the banners and crowds. Whatif had managed to convince me. Not for long, but still.

On that day of *mine*, my first and only, the noise and parti-colored light from a mass demonstration had been beating against my lenses and brain since morning. For a minute I even put away my inseparable adjunct: spots whirled round me, dancing a haphazard jig. The sun skipped in the March puddles. In the rain-washed March azure, white cloud-blots pranced.

For want of habit, I very quickly tired. With vibrating nerves, nearly drunk from the sounds and meanings, so new and so *not mine*, I quietly disengaged myself from the crowd and walked along the streets. But the streets, also noisy and excited, gave my nerves no rest. Then a long cemetery enclosure met my eye. I turned in.

But strangely, the peace locked inside those walls that day was somehow unpeaceful. Crosses were pitched towards the ground and waving their crosspieces as though mounting a defense; the stone enclosure circling the cemetery resembled a fortress wall awaiting a siege.

Worn out, I sat down on a still-damp bench. It was then I caught sight of *her*: a little girl of three or four. Coming towards me down a path. She appeared to be alone. Her little legs, wobbling slightly on the hard slippery earth, were stubbornly, step by step, conquering the space. From beneath a light knitted bonnet, a fine and seemingly familiar oval shone white. The wind ruffled her golden curls and the ends of the red ribbon in which they were tied. When the little girl reached the empty end of my bench, I said:

"Life."

She knew that I meant her. Standing among the crosses, their dead white arms spread wide above her, she looked up at me and smiled. Her pupils, I noticed, were strangely dilated inside their fine blue rims.

From around a bend in the path came the sound of hastening footsteps. A woman's voice called the child. But not by the name I had given her. I quickly got up and rushed away in the opposite direction, faster and faster. Somewhere near the exit I knocked a devout old woman off her feet.

"You owl!" she cried after me.

"Comrade Owl," someone's merry bass corrected her and began to laugh.

I laughed too.

As soon as I got home, I began hunting for that long-forgotten missive. I especially needed the nine letters — helpless and touching, as it seemed to me now — that had grown up into my name: over the envelope. I dug through all my paper piles. As I searched, old useless jottings kept thrusting themselves into my hands, academic university junk, tattered book extracts, official letters. The one thing I needed was not there. The small narrow envelope with the jumping lines hidden inside had disappeared. Apparently for good.

That day, though, I was in luck; I had not disturbed the dust inside my folders and paper piles for nothing. My attention was suddenly caught by an old excerpt. A note in the margin read: *From the questions of one Kirik to Novogorod Bishop Nifont.*

And further down:

Question 41: *Ought a burial to take place after sunset?*

Answer: *No. For it is the crowning glory of the dead to see the sun at the hour of their burial.*

I went to the window and flung it wide to the night. The day noises, now abated, tossed softly and sleepily among a myriad lights. I drew a chair up to the windowsill and sat the whole night with my head in my hands. Between my temples, the thought fought and fought and would not be still: so I'm a corpse. So I am. But I too shall be given *to see the sun at the hour of my burial.*

Meanwhile the March fury was rising higher and higher. Many felt frightened by its violent surge. What happened was what had to happen. At first the dead and the living lived together. And life, caught fast, fettered, and forced to become a dead mechanism monotonously counting off the days, seemed to favor the dead. They were more convenient for the *foundation* and the *structure* that then existed. Later on, the war separated, at least in part, the dead from the living: having finished with the living, having settled accounts with them for good, the war wanted to give life to galvanized corpses. But the living, herded into the slaughterhouse, found themselves *together* for the first time and thereby *took hold of Life*. They didn't need to produce it by galvanic means, by stealing things from nature: nature was right there in them — inside their nerves and muscles. An ordinary constitution of muscles tore down the walls of the splendidly equipped slaughterhouse — and there began the only fight in the annals of the planet or, rather, the only revolt of *the living against the dead*.

The Revolution, as I see it, was not an internecine war between Reds and Whites, Greens and Reds, not a campaign of East against West, class against class, but quite simply a fight for the planet between Life and Death. Either — or.

When the Revolution began to get the upper hand, then, of course, corpses too got involved: all those "and I"s, "half-I"s, "barely I"s, and "slightly I"s. And especially that variety of corpse that I had discovered: "to me". They offered life experience, work experience, knowledge, passivity, compassion and loyalty. Everything except: life. Yet it was life that was mainly in demand. It gradually became clear that, outside cemeteries too, there was ample room for corpses. The Revolution knew how to "use" them. A doctor of my acquaintance once told me about the symptoms of something called climacterium. During the climacteric period, he explained, a woman's sexual system grows gradually numb, losing sensitivity and the physiological sensation of love. Climacteric women cannot love (purely physiologically). But they can be loved. Taking this example *in extenso*, I maintain that people with a numb sensorium, with an almost corpse-like ossification of the psyche, can no longer live themselves. But they can be lived. Why not?

I may be climacteric too, but *I've understood*. I cannot live. And I feel ashamed: because I saw, if only for an instant, the sun at the hour of my burial.

One day this past summer, I was walking along the banks of the Moscow River and noticed some boys playing skittles. The game was in full swing.

I stopped to watch.

"Hey, Petka, set up the dead man," a bold boy's voice rent the air.

Petka, bare soles flashing, dashed inside the square etched in the dirt and quickly arranged the skittles: two lay side by side — the table. A third on top: the corpse. And two more flanking them, upright: the candles.

"Right, and now..." Petka ran back to the line and picked up the bat. For a second he fixed the "dead man" with a squinting, slightly malicious eye. Then the bat hurtled through the air, and the dead man flew helter-skelter out of his square. A cloud of dust rose up over him then settled back down again.

I thought to myself: it's time. It's now time.

And indeed: *Dasein-Ersatz* — imitation life — used to be possible. But now it's harder. Almost impossible.

New eyes have appeared. And people. They have a new way of looking at you: *not at, but through*. You can't hide your emptiness inside: they will bore into you with their pupils. No need to move aside when you meet them: they will walk right through you, as through air.

I feel sorry for all those "and I"s and "barely I"s still clinging to their half-existence: living for them is hard and tedious: *no* has driven a wedge *into yes*; *left* has run *into right*; the top of their life is stove in, and shielding itself with the bottom. Even so they will all, no matter where they hide, be dragged out and opened up like old tin cans that have rusted through: better to bury *oneself* away beneath a dark blue lid with white trim.

A month ago I had an encounter. I was walking along the Arbat, past shop windows; in the windows were numbers on tags; under the tags were goods; but in one window, above the number, were two bullet holes caulked with a muddy gray paste. Which struck me as curious: I lingered for a moment. And suddenly heard a merry voice at my ear:

"You're intrigued. Y-yes, skillfully mended. Here we've riddled all of Russia with bullets, but she... again. Has been mended..." the voice broke off.

A couple absorbed in studying the numbers — arm in arm — walked quietly away. I ventured a glance: from under a leathern cap, sharp pupils with a nickel shine; a clean-shaven face wedged between high knobby cheekbones; a scar across the forehead.

"Here we see," the man went on, "how greedy people are for things. And though they can't buy them, they can at least feast their eyes. Well I don't need any of that," he flicked a square, stubby-fingered hand, "which is why I travel like a bullet: either past or through. I also have a rule: that all my belongings weigh no more than 11½ pounds."

"Why 11½?" I asked.

"Because with a rifle the weight is determined: 11½

pounds, and that's all. So as not to overbalance the rifle's bayonet. Understand?"

I nodded. We ambled down the street, and turned in at the first beer sign we saw. The details are still fresh in my mind: on the wall, above our table, inside a square frame, a ship, its hull upturned over a dark blue and white sea, was sinking. Beneath the ship, along a paper band, ran four widely spaced letters: from right to left, they read: I-K-A-R. [Icarus], and from left to right: R-A-K-I [crayfish].*

From every quarter: *that*.

We asked for two beers. I barely touched the foam on mine. He drained his at one draught. And went on talking while looking somewhere through me.

"Eleven holes I've got in me, but I don't want to die. Life interests me too much. Take the time they picked me up near Saratov — we were fighting the Czechs there — with barely any blood left in me: it had all run out. They said I'd die. But not me, oh no, I just didn't believe it is all. Then there was the time the Whites caught me. Lined us up along the edge of a ravine. As soon as I heard the word: 'Re-e-eady!' — I dropped like a stone, rolled down the incline and ran. They gave chase: bang-bang. But I kept on, I somehow knew that they'd never hit me. How could they? How could they hit a man who can't possibly do without life?"

This acquaintance (I didn't often allow myself the luxury) was not cut short. The man in the leathern cap even came to my room: for the books. With me, the books' owner, he,

---

* Crayfish are a typical Russian accompaniment to beer. (*Tr.*)

apparently, had no business. He never once asked me who I was or what was in me. But my books he devoured. To start with I gave him a bundle of simpler things. He won't understand, I thought. No. He understood. In his own way, but he understood. Then I gave him other books: more difficult ones. On returning the second bundle to me, he divided the books into two piles.

"These went past. Those went through."

When my guest had gone I looked through each of the two piles, taking care not to mix them up: very interesting.

By the way, you too may make the acquaintance of this acquaintance of mine (if you like), as the delivery of my manuscript shall be entrusted to him. At our last meeting I told him that I was going away. Tomorrow, as agreed, I shall give him the packet so that in exactly a week it may be delivered to Room No. 24. I can rely on him. Of that I'm sure.

In the interim period between the two Romes (now both dead) the game of *cottabus* was very much in vogue. The object was this: when guests had finished feasting they would fling the last drops of wine from the last goblets to see who could fling them the furthest. Both periods and games, it seems, recur. Well then, I, a drop, accept the game. We're on. Hurl me. But not the goblet. The empty goblet must remain where it is: those are the rules of the "game of cottabus".

Well, it's time I finished: both my manuscript, and everything. People are up next door. The day is beginning. So then, I must: drop off the manuscript; dispose of my books and effects; then destroy various papers. That will take the better part of a day and perhaps a night. Fine. Then lock the door and throw the key out the window, into the snow. To be on the safe side. Now let's see... yes, the hook is in the wall (I hammered it in yesterday) — in the third rose to the horizontal right of the doorjamb. Its story is clear, as is mine. Until the first glimmers, the hook will be bare. Then not bare. By the way, I've already experimented with a chair, purposely knocking it over with a clatter. The first time someone yelled through the wall: "What's going on?" The second time they didn't bother. So on this point I'm guaranteed. Twenty-fours hours will go by, perhaps more, and the hook will still not be bare. Then someone will call to me through the door. Then they'll knock. Softly at first; then more loudly. Three or four people will gather by the door: first they'll bang on it, then they'll stop. Then they'll take an axe to the lock. They'll walk in. Jump back. And walk in again, only not all of them. They'll unburden the hook, then pull it out of the wall. After that, room No. 24 will remain empty for a day, or two, or even three, until it admits you.

I'm afraid that by now you must be feeling somewhat anxious. Don't be afraid: I won't menace you with hallucinations. Those are cheap psychological tricks. I'm counting instead on that exceedingly prosaic law: *the association of ideas and images*. Even now, everything — from the flat blue blots on the wallpaper to the last letters on these pages — has entered your brain. I'm already fairly well entangled in your "associative threads"; I've already seeped into your "I". Now you too have a *figment*.

Be warned: science has proven that attempts to

disentangle associative threads and excise the foreign image only embed that image more firmly in one's consciousness. After all those failed experiments with my "I", my dream has been to ensconce myself at least in someone else's. If you are at all alive, I have *already succeeded*. Goodbye."

The lines broke off. Shtamm's eyes continued to skim down the copybook's empty blue rules for another second or two. Then they stopped short.

Shtamm turned his face to the door. He stood up. To the door it was six steps. Third to the right: yes, his fingers clearly felt a narrow hole.

Suddenly he jerked open the door and rushed out. But his fingers ran straight into the corridor wall. The corridor was quiet and dark. Save for the narrow band of light from Shtamm's half-open door. It helped him to see: in front of his eyes a number showed white: 25. For a minute he stood stock-still, he wanted to hear a living sound: if only the sound of human breathing. The people behind that closed door were probably asleep: Shtamm pressed his ear to the number and listened. But he heard only his own blood, chafing against his veins.

Gradually regaining his self-possession, he turned back: to his threshold. He walked in and closed the door tight behind him. Again he sat down at the table. The manuscript was waiting. Shtamm pushed it aside and covered it with a book. On top of the book he placed his briefcase. The black night hush still hovered. Then suddenly (in Moscow this happens), somewhere nearby, a bell tower started from its sleep: ringing at random, but with brio, bells banging mightily against the silence. And just as suddenly, it stopped. The disconcerted copper droned on for a minute more in a low, slow-fading monotone — and then again the hush closed in. Little by little the day began to dawn. The dove-colored half-light clinging to the panes crept slowly into the room. Shtamm moved to the window. His agitation was gradually subsiding. Now through the frozen double panes he could see: the iron hulls of upturned roof-ships plunging slowly into the dawn; the rows of black window holes beneath them; and the crooked cracks of side-streets down below; the cracks were deserted, dead and mute.

"*His hour,*" Shtamm whispered, and felt as though a noose was tightening about his throat.

From far away, from the outskirts, came the long even bass of an automobile horn.

"I wonder if that man will turn up again: the alive one."

Now Shtamm was again — or so it seemed to him — his old self; even almost Etal.

Only now he noticed that the dark blue roses on the wall were encased in a thin — thread-thin — white border.

"What of it?" Shtamm muttered, sinking into a reverie. "Can't very well find another room. I'll have to stay here. And besides, I don't care *what* I'll have to do."

*1925*

# The Unbitten Elbow

This whole story would have remained hidden inside the sleeve and starched cuff of a jacket, if not for the *Weekly Review*. The *Weekly Review* came up with a questionnaire — Your favorite writer? Your average weekly earnings? Your goal in life? — and sent it out to all subscribers. The deluge of completed questionnaires (the *Review* had a huge circulation) included one, Blank No. 11111, which, wander as it did through sorters' fingers, could not be found a suitable folder: on Blank No. 11111, opposite "Average Earnings", the respondent had written "0", and opposite "Goal in Life", in clear round letters, "To bite my elbow".

The blank was sent for clarification to the secretary; from the secretary it went before the round, black-rimmed glasses of the editor. The editor jabbed his call button, a messenger scurried in then scurried out — and a minute later the blank, folded in four, slipped into the pocket of a reporter, who had received verbal instructions as well:

"Talk to him in a slightly playful tone and try to understand the point: What is this? Symbolism or romantic irony? Well, anyway, you know what I mean..."

The reporter assumed a knowing expression and set

out promptly for the address given at the bottom of the blank.

A tram took him as far as the last, suburban stop; then the zigzags of a narrow staircase led him at length to an attic; finally, he knocked on a door and waited for an answer. But none was forthcoming. Another knock, more waiting — and the reporter gave the door a push. It yielded and his eyes met this scene: a penurious room, walls crawling with bedbugs, a table and a wooden stove-bench. On the table, an unfastened cuff; on the stove-bench, a man, his arm bared, his mouth edging towards the crook of his elbow.

Absorbed in his task, the man clearly had not heard the knocks on the door or the steps on the stair; only the intruder's loud voice made him raise his head. Here the reporter descried on No. 11111's arm, a few inches from the sharp elbow pointing in his direction, several scratches and tooth marks. Unable to bare the sight of blood, he turned away and said:

"You seem to be in earnest, that is, I mean, there's no symbolism here is there?"

"None."

"And I suppose romantic irony hasn't got anything to do with it either..."

"Pure anachronism," the elbow-eater muttered, returning to the scratches and scars with his mouth.

"Stop! Oh, stop!" the reporter cried, shutting his eyes. "When I've gone, go right ahead. But for the moment won't you allow your mouth to give me a short interview? Tell me, have you been at this long?" his pencil began scratching in his notebook.

When he had finished, the reporter walked out the door then came right back:

"Listen, trying to bite your own elbow's all very well, but you know it can't be done. No one has ever succeeded; every attempt has ended in failure. Has it occurred to you that you are a strange person?"

In response: two glazed eyes beneath knitted brows and a curt:

"*El possibile esta para los toutos.*"*

The clapped-shut notebook opened again.

"Forgive me, I'm not a linguist. Would you mind..."

But No. 11111, evidently unable to bear the separation any longer, had reapplied his mouth to his badly bitten arm, while the reporter, tearing his eyes and whole body away, turned on his heels and sprinted down the zigzag stairs, hailed a motor and raced back to the office. The next issue of the *Weekly Review* ran an item headlined: "*El Possibile Esta Para Los Toutos*".

Adopting a slightly playful tone, the piece described a naive crackpot, whose naivety bordered on... On what, the *Review* did not say, ending instead with the pithy dictum of a forgotten Portuguese philosopher, intended to chasten and check all the sociopathic dreamers and fanatics searching in our realistic and sober century for the impossible and impracticable. This mysterious dictum, which also appeared in the headline, was followed by a brief: "*sapienti sat.*"**

---

* *Mangled Span.* Es possible esto para todos. Anyone can do it.
** A sage is satisfied (*Lat.*).

Random readers of the *Weekly Review* expressed interest in this bizarre case, two or three magazines picked up on it — and soon it would have receded in memories and archives if not for the attack on the *Weekly Review* by the weightier *Monthly Review*. The next issue of that organ ran an item: "Without a Leg to Stand On". The caustic author quoted the *Weekly Review* then noted that the Portuguese dictum was in fact a Spanish proverb and that its meaning was this: "Any fool can do it". To this the author added a terse "*et insapienti sat*"*, and to that short "*sat*" a tight-laced "(*sic*)".

After which the *Weekly Review* had no choice but to explain — in a very long piece in the very next issue, fighting "*sat*" with "*sat*" — that not everyone is blessed with a sense of irony: to be pitied, of course, was not this naive attempt to do the undoable (all genius, after all, is naive), not this fanatic of his own elbow, but that mercenary hireling, that creature in blinkers from the *Monthly Review*, who, as he dealt only with letters, understood everything literally.

Now the *Monthly Review* wanted to retaliate, but the *Weekly Review* could not let it have the last word. In the bitter debate that ensued, the elbow fanatic came across as a cretin and a genius by turns, a candidate for an insane asylum one day and the Academy of Sciences the next.

As a result, several hundred thousand readers of both reviews learned of No. 11111 and his attitude towards his elbow. Among the public at large, however, this debate did

---

* An idiot is satisfied (*Lat.*).

not elicit much interest, especially given other, more compelling events: two earthquakes and one chess match: every day two thickheaded fellows sat down to 64 squares — one with the face of a butcher, the other with that of a clerk in a chic shop — and somehow fellows and squares were the focus of everyone's intellectual interests, needs and expectations. Meanwhile, No. 11111, in his small square room, not unlike a chess square, his elbow pulled up to his jaw, waited, wooden and inert, like a dead chess piece, to be put in play.

The first person to make the elbow-eater a serious offer was the manager of a suburban circus in search of new acts to enliven the show. He was an enterprising sort, and an old issue of the *Review*, on which his eyes happened to light, decided the elbow-eater's immediate fate. The poor devil refused at first, but when the showman pointed out that this was the only way to make his elbow his bread and butter, and that a living wage would allow him to refine his method and improve his professional technique, the lachrymose crackpot mumbled something like "uh-huh".

This act — billed as *Elbow vs. Man. Will he or won't he bite it? Three 2-minute rounds. Referee Belks* — was the finale, after the Lady with the Python, the Roman Gladiators and the Jump from Under the Dome. It went like this: with the orchestra playing a march, a man walked out into the arena with one arm bared; his cheeks were rouged, the scars around his funny bone meticulously powdered and whitened. The orchestra stopped playing — and the contest began: the man's teeth sank into his forearm and began edging towards his elbow, little by little, closer and closer.

"Bluffer, you won't bite it!"

"Look, look! I think he bit it."

"No, he didn't. So near and yet so..."

Yet the champion's neck, veins bulging, continued to strain and stretch, his eyes, glued to his elbow, turned bloodshot, blood dripped from his bites onto the sand, while increasingly frantic spectators brandishing binoculars jumped out of their seats, stamped their feet, climbed over barricades, hooted, whistled and screamed:

"Grab it with your teeth!"

"Come on, catch that elbow!"

"Hang on, elbow! Don't give in!"

"No fair! They're in cahoots!"

After three rounds, the referee announced the elbow the winner. And neither the referee, nor the impresario, nor the departing crowd suspected that for the man with the bared elbow the circus arena would soon give place to the arena of world acclaim, that instead of a sandy circle — some 20 yards in diameter — he would have at his feet the earth's ecliptic, swinging its radiuses over thousands of miles.

Here is how it all began: the popular speaker Eustace Kint, risen to fame through the ears of old but wealthy ladies, was taken by friends — by chance, after a merry birthday lunch — to the circus. A professional philosopher, Kint caught the elbow-eater's metaphysical meaning right off the bat. The very next morning he began an article on "The Principles of Unbiteability".

Kint, who only a few years before had trumped the tired motto "Back to Kant" with the new and now current "Forward to Kint", wrote with elegant ease and rhetorical flourishes. (Small wonder: it was he, after all, who had once said, to thunderous applause, that "philosophers, when speaking to people about the world, see the world, but they do not see that their listeners, located in that same world, not ten feet away from them, are bored to tears.") After a vivid description of "Man vs. Elbow", Kint generalized the contest and, hypostatizing it, pronounced this circus act *metaphysics in action.*

The philosopher's thinking went like this: any concept (*Begriff*, in the language of the great German metaphysicians) comes lexically and logically from *greifen*, which means, "to grasp, to grip, to bite". But any *Begriff*, when carried to its logical conclusion, becomes a *Grenzbegriff*, or "limit-concept", which is beyond comprehension, unable to be grasped by the mind, just as one's elbow is unable to be grasped by one's teeth. "Furthermore," Kint reasoned, "in objectifying the unbiteable externally, we arrive at the idea of the transcendent. Kant understood this very well. But he did not understand that the transcendent is also immanent (*manus* — 'hand', hence, also, 'elbow'); the immanent-transcendent is always in the 'here', extremely close to the comprehensible and almost part of the apperception apparatus, just as one's elbow is almost within reach of the grasping efforts of one's jaws. But the elbow is 'so near and yet so far', and the 'thing-in-itself' is in every self, yet ungraspable. Here we have an intransgressible *almost*," Kint concluded, "an 'almost' that is personified, as it were, by the man in the sideshow trying very hard to bite his own elbow. Alas, every round inevitably ends in victory for the elbow: the man is defeated — the transcendent triumphs. Again and again — to howls and roars from the boorish crowd — we are treated to a crude, but brilliant version of the age-old gnoseological drama. Go one, go all, hurry to the tragic sideshow, ponder this most remarkable phenomenon: for a few coins you will be given that for which the flower of humanity paid with their lives."

Kint's tiny black type proved far more effective than the huge red letters on circus posters. Crowds flocked to see the dirt-cheap metaphysical wonder. The elbow-eater's act had to be moved from its suburban tent to a theater in the center of the city, where No. 11111 began performing at universities as well. Kintists now took to quoting and discussing their teacher's ideas. As for Kint, he turned his article into a book: *Elbowism: Premises and Deductions*. Its first year, it went through 43 editions.

The number of elbowists was mushrooming. True, skeptics and anti-elbowists had also cropped up; an elderly professor tried to prove the antisocial nature of the elbowist movement, a throwback, he claimed, to Stirnerianism, which would logically lead to solipsism, that is to say, to a philosophical dead end.

The movement also had its more serious detractors. Thus a columnist by the name of Tnik, while speaking at a conference on problems of elbowism, asked: But what if the celebrated elbow-eater should finally manage to bite his own elbow?

Tnik was hissed and dragged off the stage before he could finish. The poor wretch didn't ask for the floor again.

And then there were the envious pretenders; thus one self-promoter announced in print that on such-and-such a day at such-and-such a time he had succeeded in biting his elbow. A verifying committee was sent straight out, the imposter exposed, and soon, dogged by contempt and outrage, he committed suicide.

This incident only increased No. 11111's fame: students at universities where he had performed trooped around after him, especially the girls. One of the loveliest — with the sad shy eyes of a gazelle — obtained a private meeting so as to offer up her half-bared arms in sacrifice:

"If you feel you must, bite mine: it's certainly easier."

But her eyes were stopped by two murky blurs cowering beneath black brows. In response she heard:

"Do not gore what is not yours."

Whereupon the glum fanatic of his own elbow turned away, giving the girl to understand that the audience was over.

Nevertheless, No. 11111 remained the rage. A well-known wag understood the number 11111 to mean that the man it designated was "singular five times over". Men's clothing stores began selling special-cut jackets — known as "elbowets" — with a flap that unbuttoned to allow the wearer, whenever and wherever, to try his hand at biting his elbow. Many elbowist converts gave up drinking and smoking. Fashionable ladies began wearing high-necked, long-sleeved dresses with round cutouts at the elbows and decorating their funny bones with elegant red appliques imitating fresh bites and scratches. A venerable Hebraist, having devoted forty years to uncovering the real dimensions of Solomon's temple, now retracted his findings: he confessed that the verse in the Bible that says "the length thereof" was 60 cubits should instead be read as a symbol of the 60-fold ungraspableness of what is hidden beyond the veil. In an effort to gain popularity, a parliamentary deputy drafted a bill to abolish the metric system in favor of that ancient, elbow-conscious measure: the cubit. And although the bill was ultimately defeated, the raucous discussions it prompted in parliament, to say nothing of the two duels, made sensational daily news.

Having gripped the broad masses, elbowism became vulgarized and lost the strict philosophical aspect Kint had attempted to give it. Cheap sheets, misinterpreting elbowist teachings, promoted it with slogans like "Elbow Your Way to the Top", "Rely on Your Elbows and Your Elbows Alone".

Soon this warped new trend in elbowist thought had become so wildly widespread that the State, which counted No. 11111 a citizen, naturally decided to use him for its own budgetary purposes. An opportunity was not long in presenting itself. Elbow mania had already prompted certain sporting publications to print regular bulletins on the quarter-inches and eighth-inches still separating the elbow-eater's teeth from his elbow. Now a semi-official government paper began printing similar bulletins on the next-to-last page, between the trotting-race results, soccer scores and stock market reports. Some time later, this same semi-official paper ran a piece by a famous academician, a proponent of Neo-Lamarckism. Proceeding from the assumption that the organs of a living organism evolve by means of exercise, he concluded that the elbow was, in theory, *biteable*. Given a gradual stretching of the neck's cross-striated muscular matter, this authority wrote, a systematic twisting of the forearm, etc... With that, the logically impeccable Kint struck the academician a blow for unbiteability. The argument that ensued recalled Spencer's with the dead Kant. The time was now ripe: a bankers' trust (everyone knew its shareholders included government bigwigs and the country's top capitalists) sent out fliers announcing a Grand BTE (Bite That Elbow) Lottery to be held every Sunday. The trust promised to pay every ticket holder 11,111 monetary units to one (to ONE!) as soon as the elbow-eater's elbow was bitten.

The lottery was launched with much fanfare — jazz bands and iridescent Chinese lanterns. "Wheels of fortune" began spinning. The ticket ladies' white teeth, grinning in welcome, and bare red-flecked elbows, diving inside glass globes full of tickets, toiled from midday to midnight.

But ticket sales were sluggish at first. The idea of unbiteability was too firmly ingrained in people's minds. The ancient Lamarckist called on Kint, but Kint continued to demur:

"The Lord God Himself," he declared at one of their meetings, "cannot arrange things so that two and two do not equal four, so that a man can bite his own elbow, and thought can transgress the bounds of the limit-concept."

The number of so-called biteableists, who championed this new venture, was, compared to that of unbiteableists, insignificant and shrinking every day; lottery bonds were tumbling, depreciating to almost nothing. The voices of Kint and his adherents — demanding that the masterminds behind this scam be exposed, that the parliament resign, that reforms be instituted — sounded louder and louder. But then one night Kint's apartment was searched and his desk found to contain a fat stack of lottery tickets. The order for his arrest was instantly revoked, the discovery made public, and by day's end the stock price for tickets had begun to climb.

Avalanches they say, may begin like this: a raven, perched high on a mountain peek, beats its wing against the snow, a lump of which goes sliding down the slope, gathering ever-more snow as it goes; rocks and earth go crashing after it — debris and more debris — until the avalanche, furrowing the mountainside, has engulfed and flattened everything in its path. So: a raven beats its wing then turns its hunched back on the consequences, pulls scales over its eyes and goes to sleep; the avalanche's roar wakes the bird; it pulls the scales from its eyes, straightens its back, and beats the other wing. The biteableists supplanted the unbiteableists; the river of events reversed itself, flowing from mouth to source. Elbowets were now to be seen only in rag-and-bone shops. Meanwhile No. 11111, that lottery-ticket wonder, that living guarantee of capital investment, went on public view. Thousands upon thousands of people filed past the glass cage in which he now labored round the clock. This buoyed hopes and increased sales. As did the semi-official bulletins, now run on the front page in large print: every time they shaved off another fraction of an inch, tens of thousands more tickets were snapped up.

The elbow-eater's determination — inspiring universal belief in the attainability of the unattainable, swelling the ranks of biteableists everywhere — rattled even the stock market. Briefly. One day the fractions of an inch separating mouth and elbow so diminished (triggering yet another surge in ticket sales) that the government called a secret emergency meeting: what if the impossible were to happen and the elbow were to be bitten? To redeem even a tenth of all the tickets, at the advertised rate of 11,111 to 1, said the finance minister, would leave the State to tatters. The trust president put it this way: "A tooth in his elbow would mean a knife in our throat: revolution without fail. But short of a miracle, that will not happen. Remain calm."

And indeed, the next day the fractions of an inch began to increase. The elbow-eater seemed to be losing ground to his triumphant elbow. Then something unexpected happened: the elbow-eater's mouth, like a leech that has sucked its fill, let go of his bloodied arm, and for an entire week the man in the glass cage, glazed eyes to the ground, did not renew his struggle.

The metal turnstiles by the cage turned faster and faster, thousands upon thousands of anxious eyes streamed past the dephenomenoned phenomenon, the hue and cry grew louder every day. Ticket sales stopped. Fearing unrest, the government increased the number of policemen on duty tenfold, while the trust increased the return on subscription tickets.

Special keepers, assigned to look after No. 11111, tried to sick him on his own elbow (as one would an animal that resists its trainer: with iron prods); but the elbow-eater only snarled and turned gloomily away from the food he had clearly grown to hate. The stiller the man in the glass cage became, the greater the commotion around him. And who knows where it would all have led, if not for this: one day before dawn, when the guards and keepers, having despaired of ever getting elbow and man to fight again, took their eyes off No. 11111, he suddenly fell on his enemy. Behind those glazed eyes the past week, something thought-like had plainly been occurring and prompted new tactics. Now the elbow-eater, attacking his elbow from the rear, rushed straight for it — through the flesh in the crook of his arm. Hacking through the layers with his hook-like jaws, his face awash in blood, he had nearly reached the inside of his elbow. But just before that bony junction, as we know, comes the confluence of three arteries: *arteriae brachialis, radialis et ulnaris*. From this severed arterial knot, blood now began to gush and fountain, leaving the elbow-eater's body limp and lifeless. His teeth — a hair from the prize — came unhooked, his arm straightened out, and his hand fell to the ground — followed by his entire body.

His keepers heard the noise and reached the cage in time to find No. 11111, sprawled in a spreading pool of blood, stone-dead.

Insofar as the earth and its rotational devices continued

to turn on their axes, the story of the man who wanted to bite his elbow does not, of course, end here. The story, but not the fairy tale: here the two — the Fairy Tale and the Story — part ways. The Story steps — not for the first time — over the body and goes on, but the Fairy Tale is a superstitious old woman and afraid of bad omens. Please don't blame her and don't judge her too harshly.

*1927*

# The Bookmark

1

The other day, as I was looking through my old books and manuscripts tied tight with twine, it again slipped under my fingers: a flat body of faded blue silk and needlepoint designs finished with a double-wedge train. We hadn't seen each other in a long time: my bookmark and I. Events of recent years had been too unbookish and had taken me far from those cabinets crammed with herbariumized meanings. I abandoned the bookmark between lines as yet unread and soon forgot the feel of its slippery silk and the delicate scent of printing ink emanating from its soft and pliant body wafered between the pages, I even forgot... where I had forgotten it. Thus do long sea voyages part sailors from their wives.

True, books had crossed my path here and there: rarely at first, then more and more often; but they did not need bookmarks. These were unraveling signatures glued pell-mell into crookedly cut covers; along the rough and dirty paper, breaking ranks with the lines, brown-gray letters — the color of military broadcloth — rushed; these reeked of rancid oil and glue. With these crudely produced bareheaded bundles, one did not stand on ceremony: shoving a finger in between the sloppily pasted signatures, one tore the pages apart the better to leaf through them, tugging impatiently at the raggedy, tooth-edged margins. One consumed these texts posthaste, without reflecting or delectating: both books and two-wheeled carts were needed then strictly to supply words and ammunition. The one with the silk train had no business here.

And now again: the ship was in port, its gangway down. Library ladders scanning the spines of books. The statics of frontispieces. Silence and green reading-room lampshades. Pages rubbing against pages. And, finally, the bookmark: just as it had been, all that time ago — except that now the silk was even more faded, and its needlepoint design covered in dust.

I pulled it out from under a paper mound and placed it in front of me — on the edge of the desk: the bookmark looked affronted and slightly grumpy. But I smiled at it with warmth and affection: to think of all the voyages we had taken together — from meanings to meanings, from this set of signatures to that. Now, for instance, I recalled our difficult ascent from ledge to ledge of Spinoza's *Ethics* — after almost every page I had left my bookmark alone, squeezed between the metaphysical layers; then the breathlessness of *Vita nuova* where, at passages linking one poem to the next, my patient bookmark had often had to wait until the emotion that had taken the book out of my hands subsided, allowing me to return to the words. And I couldn't I help remembering... But all of this concerns only the two of us, me and my bookmark: I'll stop.

Especially as it is important in practice — in that any encounter obligates — to repay the past given us with some bit of the future. In other words, rather than tucking the bookmark away at the back of a drawer, I should include my old friend in my next reading; instead of a series of memories, I should offer my guest another bundle of books.

I looked through what I had. No, none of these would do: they lacked the logical caesuras and dramatic shifts that force one to look back and to pause, that call for the help of a bookmark. I ran my eye over the freshly printed titles: in that jumble of meager contrivances there was nowhere to stop. No corner to be found for my four-cornered guest.

I looked away from the bookshelf and tried to remember: empty literary boxcars of the last few years clattered though my mind. Here too I could see no place for my bookmark. Somewhat irritated, I first paced — from wall to wall — and then, arms thrust into the sleeves of my overcoat, went out for my usual late afternoon walk.

2

I am billeted at the bend in the Arbat, cater-corner to the church of St. Nicholas, so the boulevards are only a few hundred paces away: first I pass the window of the second-hand store walled off by the backs of gawkers, then I follow the sidewalk — past doors and signs — straight to the square. This time too an absurd habit, left over from the long-forgotten hungry years, made me stop to peer in the window of a food shop: through the cloudy glass, those same defenseless, pimply chicken legs sticking out of greasy paper peered back with dead pomp.

I tore my eyes away and proceeded along the pavement through the polygon of Arbat Square to Nikitsky Boulevard; through another square, more packed boulevard sand — and I began to look for a free place on some bench or other. One bench, with a slumped-back back and squat, bent-iron legs, had room at one end. I sat down, shoulder to someone's shoulder, intending to finish thinking about what I'd begun at home, amongst my books and bookmark. But on this bench someone was already thinking — what's more out loud: he was second on my right; turned towards the man seated between us, the stranger went on talking. Squinting in the speaker's direction, I glimpsed only fingers fidgeting with an unbuttoned coat-breast, as with the neck of a cello (the rest was hidden by the tall and stout figure of the man being addressed).

"Or take this. I call it 'The Tower Gone Mad'. The gigantic four-footed Eiffel Tower, its steel head high over the human hubbubs of Paris, was fed up, you see, fed up with having to listen to that hurly-burly street-entangled life strewn with clangs, lights, and clamor. As for the muddleheaded creatures swarming at its feet, they had equipped the inside of its pointed crown poking through the clouds with global vibrations and radio signals. The space inside the tower's needle-like brain now began to vibrate, began to seep down through its muscular steel interlacements into the ground, whereupon the tower wrenched its iron soles free of the foundation, rocked back and lunged off. This happened before dawn, let's say, when people were asleep under their roofs, and the Place des Invalides, the Champs de Mars, adjacent streets and quays were deserted. The thousand-foot colossus, barely able to lift its heavy swollen feet, crashes across the cast-iron arc of a bridge, circumvents the sad stones of the Trocadéro and lumbers up the rue d'Iéna towards the Bois de Boulogne: in that narrow defile of houses, the tower feels ill-at-ease, once or twice it knocks into sleeping walls, houses crack and crumble, spilling bricks and waking neighbors. Less frightened than embarrassed by its clumsiness, the tower lurches into the next street. But in this still narrower defile, it has no room at all. Meanwhile, Paris the light sleeper is waking: projector lights striate the night fog, anxious sirens blare, and high overhead engines are already droning. The tower now lifts its flat elephantine feet and jumps up onto the rooftops; roof beams crackle under the Eiffel monster's leaden tread; multiplying catastrophes as it goes, it soon reaches the edge of the Bois and, cutting a wide swath with steel blows, continues on its way.

"Daylight is beginning to glimmer. Thrown into a panic, Paris's three million have jammed all the train stations; news of the tower gone mad is pounding off the presses, skimming over the wires, skipping from ear to ear. The sun climbs above the horizon and gives Parisians the chance, when they turn their heads at the usual angle towards the usual place where the tip of the tower always usually loomed, to see unusually empty air — and nothing else. Initially, this only adds to the uproar. Now these eyes, now those, seem to have seen the gigantic latticework, now wading towards them around bends in the Seine, now threatening to jump down on the city from Montmartre. But soon both the morning fog and the false alarms have dissipated, and millions of sanguine souls, who had reacted to the disaster by beating their shirtfronts and combing the papers, are indignant and demanding revenge: catch the runaway! Americans from hotels on the Place Monceau are out clicking their Kodaks, photographing the steel giant's tracks imprinted on bodies and wreckage, while a poet from Saint-Celestin, come on foot (so as to save ten sous) to the smashed bare base, chews a meditative pencil and debates what would best suit the situation: Alexandrine rhymes or zigzags of free verse?

"Swaying and droning in the wind, shimmering with the brilliance of its metal battens, the tower forges ahead; only the soft friable ground slows its steps. Though the runaway knows clearly *whence* it comes, it scarcely knows *where* it is going: chance propels it northwest, straight into the sea. The steel behemoth wants to turn back — but what's this? Cannons ranged in a semi-circle ready to fire. High-explosive shells attempt to bar its way; humming beneath their hits, the steel breaks through the first ring and, scattering cannons, storms north: to the formidable fortification walls of Antwerp. Batteries thunder: steel clashes against steel. Reeling from the hits, rocking on its lacerated joints, the tower screams out in an iron voice and staggers round to the southeast. Like a wild beast driven back into its cage with whips, the tower is ready to return and dig its feet back into the square people have assigned it. But just then it hears, from faraway in the east, a barely audible radio call: 'This way, this way!'

"You'd like me to move over? Certainly..."

Someone had sat down to the speaker's right, nearly flattening him: for a second his fingers stopped fiddling with his coat-breast which jutted forward; now I could see an angular profile, a scraggy beard, and a mouth twitching from words as from a tick.

"You and I, of course, know who was calling the lost tower and from where. And now it knows where to go: due east. The revolutionary will join the revolutionaries. From capital to capital the wires hum with fright: 'The mad rogue has been Bolshevized.' 'Stop the tower!' 'Shame!' 'Spare no effort.' 'Join forces.' Ranged cannons again try to bar the fugitive's way: once more the clanking colossus, battered by blows of steel against steel, bursts into its savage and terrible hymn. Riddled with shellbursts and shaking its needlelike crown, it trudges on in the direction of the summons. In its dreams, the tower can already see flags like red poppies flying over a vast — stalk to stalk — human field, it imagines a resounding square surrounded by ancient gap-toothed walls: there it will sink its iron soles into the ground while... while scattered armies retreat and clear the way. Diplomatic heads, meanwhile, are frantic: 'The tower is escaping! — We let it go. — Emergency measures. — What to do?'

"The steel giant's pursuers, half trampled beneath its heels, decide to attack its spire; having lost the battle on the ground, they move to the airwaves: antennas in Paris, New York, Berlin, Chicago, London, Rome, falsify their frequencies and plead from all sides: 'This way, this way!' They promise and lure, beckon and lie, jam voices from the east and discombobulate the tower. It wavers, unable to get its bearings, its steel head spinning. It pushes a little further east, then swings south, then changes direction again and, finally, worn out by the conflicting signals, not knowing where to go or why, follows where its invisible traces are leading. People everywhere are gloating with joy. Residents of towns and villages in the returning tower's path are temporarily evacuated while in Paris the smashed square by the Cathédrale des Invalides is quickly smoothed out and a proper ceremonial planned. But along the way, at the point where three mountainous borders meet, the tower encounters a waste of water: the stillness and depth of Lake Constance. Passing over that blue mirror, the vanquished giant catches sight of its reflection, inverted and sun-shot, with its spire pointing down. The sonorous steel shivers with disgust and, in a last paroxysm of rage, severs the invisible traces. Then it lifts its leaden paws, stands erect, and plunges (can you imagine?) crown-first from the alpine ledges. Comes the clatter of tumbling rocks and crags torn away, then, echoing from gorge to gorge, the plash of crushed waters: towering above the overflowing lake are the rigid limbs of the steel suicide. I wanted just to give you an outline, but it seems I got carried away and..."

His fingers, as if they'd finished playing the story, ran down his coat-breast and disappeared into his pocket. His eyes, too, seemed to be looking for cover. The stout man's shoulder stirred against mine.

"Well, if you tinkered with the plot, perhaps... Only you've got something wrong: the diameter of Lake Constance is fifty-five miles, so a thousand-foot-high wedge couldn't possibly cause it to overflow. And then..."

"And then: towers aren't in the habit of walking. Isn't that so?" the sharp-featured man laughed and slumped back; now even his coat-breast was eclipsed by the cumbrous figure separating us; and his voice, when he piped up again, seemed soft and indistinct.

"Look. Another theme. Up there. Do you see?"

"Where?"

"Right opposite you. Fourth floor. Last cornice on the left. A foot and a half below the window, below those smudges of whitewash. Well?"

"A ledge... I see."

"Now I'll show you a theme as well. Keep your eyes on the ledge: there it is, confined to those three feet. Can't jump, can't escape. My little theme is stuck."

Drawn into this strange game — the man being addressed, and I, and even a pair of eyeglasses that popped out suddenly from behind a newspaper at the other end of the bench — we immediately located the crosspiece that had caught the sharp-featured man's eye. Above the boulevard trees, between windows piled high in the facade of a building under reconstruction, rows of short narrow ledges jutted.

"There we have our first item; the second is — well, makes no difference to me — a tomcat, say, an ordinary vagabond tom. The result is this: driven by something — by a couple of stones thrown at it, or by hunger, suppose — our cat hustles up the zigzag stairs and through a half-open door into someone's apartment or perhaps an office where people are expected any minute... yes, an office, that will do better. Feet stamp at the tom, give chase — then fear catapults him up onto the windowsill (the window stands wide), and down onto that ledge: our exhibit is ready. Still, it wouldn't hurt — it wouldn't cost us anything — to stretch the building up past the chimney tops — from four stories to thirty — to narrow the streets, cobweb the air with wires, and set whirling below, along the tire-polished asphalt of the city-giant, hundreds and thousands of automobile wheels and seas of hurrying — eyes to the ground — businessmen.

"So: the cat vanishes out the window, two or three pairs of eyes follow it then go back to their numbers and calculations; the window claps shut; soon the workday is done and the doors too have clicked shut: the cat is alone — on a narrow strip of brick wedged into the building's stone face. The window above is quite close, but for a jump there's no room, no support: mustn't try: death. To jump down, from ledge to ledge, would be hopeless: it's too far and claws can't grip stone: death. Slowly straightening up, the tom inches along the wall: precipice. Fur bristling, green cracks of pupils hanging over the edge, he sees through the smoky air creeping blurs below; cocking an ear, he hears the incessant rumble of the streets: better wait. We are dealing, as I've said, with a cat averse to sentimental purrings, a homeless vagabond with fight-torn ears, hunger-sunken sides, and a heart well insulated against life: our hero is not afraid and does not lose his self-possession — he has been robbed of all possibilities, save that of sleep; very well — hugging the wall still closer, he closes his eyes. Here one might recount the tom's dreams, poised at a height of thirty stories, two inches from death. But let's go on. The chill evening air and perhaps hunger as well force him awake: below he sees tangles of lights, stationary and moving. He wants to stretch, to arch his back: but there's no room. His dusk-widened pupils scan the walls scored with yellow windows. Our tom, of course, doesn't realize that in one window people are arguing about the political system Europe will have a hundred years hence, in another they're listening to a lecture on a fashionable Boston religion, in a third they're poring over a chessboard, in a fourth... but to the tom, all of this (even were I to reveal it to him with the aid of some fictional device or other), all of this, I repeat, is of no use: beneath his paws is a narrow stone step, and either way, up or down: death. The sly tom again tries to hide behind his eyelids, in his dreams, but the cold seeps under his bedraggled fur, tugs at his skin and prods him awake. One by one, the windows go dark. Raindrops spatter and presently a downpour is lashing the ledge: the wet stone wants to slip out from under the tom's paws. He clings to the wall with his shivering body and cries, but the rain is banging on the canted rooftops and pounding down the downspouts: the poor tom's cries barely reach his own ears. Soon both fall silent: the rain and the cat. The last windows on the bottom floors go dark. Glistening roofs mirror the rose-colored dawn.

"Once again the sun bowls into the blue, dragging the day after it. Blinds go up. From the stone chasm below come the honks, clanks, clangs and clamor of the crowd. A passerby looks up by chance and sees a black dot far above, almost under the eaves; he squints through his eyeglasses: 'What could that be?' — but the minute hand on his watch propels him onward. Midday. Two small children, either side of a governess, whose stiff fingers they clutch, have come out for a walk. Mouths agape, they look all about them — at the wires, the walls and the cornices: 'What's that, missus?' 'Watch your step.' Thus do little people learn from big people to watch their step. The sun has dried and matted the tom's fur. A fierce hunger is knotting his intestines. He tries again to cry, but from his parched mouth comes only a rasp. The hot sun makes his eyelids droop, but nightmares instantly wake him: hanging his head over the edge of the cornice, the tom sees the floor of streets begin to sway and dance towards him — closer and closer; contracting his muscles, the tom is ready to jump when... he wakes up: the asphalt floor goes tumbling back down thirty flights — like an elevator cut loose — straight down.

"Again evening. Again yellow squares of windows. And in each one of them, long lines of words, problems, and bookmarks, patiently awaiting their pair of eyes. Once more the dead of night — the city subsides and the pavement lies bare. Pressing an ear to the stone, the solitary cat hears the hollow hum of the wires suspended between him and the asphalt.

"Another dawn. On the next ledge — not three yards from the cat's mouth — sparrows are chirping. The cat swallows his saliva and regards the twitterers with turbid eyes. The sparrows cut loose from the ledge and dive into the air.

"A fresh morning. From three floors down, from a window flung wide to the sun, comes a confused rendition of one of Metner's *Fairy Tales* or, better yet, a chorale prelude by Bach: such an august and gracious contrapuntal combination. The tom cares not a whit: he knows only the music of tin cans tied to his tail — Bach leaves him cold — and so, I regret to say, no catharsis takes place. Especially as a sudden wind slams the window shut, and the harmony with it. I must tell you that this wind, which blows in some mornings from the sea, begins as a breath but often turns into a cyclone. Now too, it first caresses the tom's crusted fur, and then, having built, tries to wrest him from the ledge. The tom has no fight left in him: filmy eyes wide, he clings to the stone with claws weak as water. The wind takes a swing and sweeps him off his paws: with a single toss, the tom goes tumbling down. His fall is briefly broken by the swaying wires below: they catch and cradle the vagabond, rocking him till the steel loops give way and let him drop, down onto the asphalt. Automobile wheels run over the body, and then a street-cleaner's cart comes by — our theme is scooped up with a metal spade and thrown onto the rubbish heap. The place where nearly all themes are thrown today, if indeed they are... *themes*."

The man to whom this story was addressed uncrossed his right leg from his left then crossed his left leg over his right. This hardly resembled a reaction. At the other end of the bench, the eyeglasses engrossed in the story of the cat jerked back. And soon their place was taken by a pair of eyes that quickly hid behind the varicolored cover of book.

Absorbed in listening, I hadn't noticed the gathering dusk. The air, now cool, rocked between the buildings: leaves twitched, dust swirled along the paths, and from somewhere — from the building site, most likely — a wood shaving skittered towards our bench: swiftly twirling, it cavorted across the boulevard and came to rest a few steps away. I noticed the intent look on the theme catcher's face as he turned the feathery, loosely curled shaving over in his hand. He gazed at it, affectionately squinting.

"Well now, and this too. Why if you straighten out its curls and look hard, there's substance enough for a short story, some ten pages. And no need to hunt for a title: 'The Shaving.' There. Then ever so carefully — spiral by spiral — something like this: a carpenter, a young fellow by the name of, say, Vaska Tyankov. He knows and loves his trade. With his axe and his plane, he will do wonders — and gladly. But the countryside is poor and work hard to come by, so Vaska Tyankov goes to the city from time to time to earn his bread. With Vaska, in his beveled wooden chest, go his chisels, axe and planes, while from there, hidden under his tools, come stowaway bundles of leaflets and proclamations. Meetings in the city take up more and more of his leisure. Events follow events. February — July — October. The Party comes out from underground, seizes power. Carpenter Vaska, long known as comrade Vasily, swaps his padlocked box of tools for a bulging briefcase fitted with a steel clasp. He's up to his ears in work: automobiles convey comrade Vasily from conference to conference, typewriters tap, telephones yap: 'Rush' — 'Priority' — 'Urgent'. Comrade

Vasily's eyelids are puffy with sleeplessness, a pencil has grown into his hand: reports, resolutions, congresses, official missions, urgent summonses. Only rarely — and timidly, dimly at that — do his dreams evoke the smoke rising over low log houses, the ripe rustling rye — and again his briefcase clicks open and clicks shut, 'have heard... have decreed', again the pencil is in his hand.

"Then one day — the most ordinary 'one day' imaginable — yet another telephone call forces Tyankov out of bed and into his boots. Sticking his briefcase under his arm, he dashes down the stairs. Outside the car is hooting. He kicks open the front door — and what does he see coming towards him, buffeted by puffs of wind, but this light shaving, curly as a ringlet and fragrant with resin. Tyankov glances about: no one (the driver is fussing with the hood). Then he quickly bends down and slips the feathery whorl into his briefcase. The hood comes down, the door slams shut, and the automobile cuts through his meetings, from entrance to entrance. Report, dissenting opinion. Another report. Someone with a slew of numbers. Tyankov wants to trump those numbers with his own. He opens his briefcase and scrabbles for the folders, but here — again — is that soft lock of a shaving. The joints of his fingers sing with a familiar sensation: between thumb and index — the plane's oblique projection, and slowly curling over his hand — the rustling ringlets, fragrant with wood and resins. Comrade Vasily is about to pull his hand back, but too late: a stippling of warm shots ripples along the nerves from his fingers to his brain, in his ear an invisible workbench creaks, under his elbow a rough board rocks, his hand is suddenly alive with the old carpenter's reflex. Government official Tyankov tries — you understand — to pick up his pencil, but his hand refuses and demands its due. The adhesive shaving is already wrapped round his index finger like a wedding ring; now not just his hand, but his entire arm, shoulder, body, tightening and tensing, are calling for the old work that was in their blood and muscles and from which they were forcibly parted. In short, the peasant in Vaska is reasserting his right to exist; he was silent for years, and might have gone on being silent if not for an insignificant shaving — and... Look at that, it's..."

We all (the whole bench) looked where his finger was pointing: as though tired of listening, the shaving, gently pushed by the wind, rolled away down the path. The wind seemed to have whisked the story away with it. But the silence lasted no more than a minute.

"Never mind. I once," the voice went on musingly, as if to itself, "stumbled over a cartridge clip. An ordinary, rain-rusted cartridge clip — from a rifle, that is. Not far from here — on the boulevard. Ground into the sand, no doubt, in the days when we talked to each other with gunshots. And here... it had turned up again. Well, I understood it right away. Right away. After all, what can a cartridge clip say: five bullets — one after another — along five trajectories and into five targets. I invented a plot along the lines of Andersen's 'Five out of One Pod' or our Russian tale about the tsarevich and his three arrows... It's not my fault if bullets are more current than those idyllic peas. So then, I took five lives, five stories in a cartridge clip, and tried... but you don't care."

His glum companion made no reply. A minute later, a passenger tram, sighing and grinding sparks, came rattling along the rails behind us.

"Or, if one were to write about one of the city's suicides — an old, but inexhaustible theme — your title would be right over there, twenty steps away, in black and white. Just turn around and copy it down."

The man being spoken to did not stir, but I glanced over my shoulder and immediately saw the title, indeed in black and white, under three red lights, on a ruled board hanging in mid-air.

"Ye-e-s," said the sharp-featured man, leaning forward with his elbows on his knees, "if I ever wanted to write about someone who put his neck in a noose or slit his throat, I would give my story a humdrum, urban title: *Flag Stop*. Yes. And if the title is right, the whole text will hang on it, like a coat on a peg. The title, for me, is the first word (or words) of a story: it must pull all the other words after it, right down to the last. That's my feeling anyway. To think that people say," he went on, suddenly raising his voice and scanning the window squares blazing up to meet the night, "that there are no themes, that we are living in a time of themelessness. They hunt for themes — practically need hounds to do it — and scare up each new series of images with a battue, a throng, when those accursed themes, the devil take them, are everywhere you look. They're like the motes in a sunbeam or the mosquitoes over a swamp — that would be more exact. Themes?! You say there aren't any. My brain is bristling with them. Asleep, or awake, from every window, from all eyes, events, things, words: they swarm: and every one, no matter how tiny, wants to sting me. Sting me! And you say..."

"I, in fact, have said nothing. And I think what you say is nonsense. We have authors..."

"*Authors?*" his scraggly beard twitched nervously. "We have no authors: we have only second-raters. Imitators. And outright thieves. How do they go about finding themes? Some scramble up sliding library ladders in pursuit — and pluck them out from under book covers. They're not so bad. But others grab them right out of each other's hands; cadge them from State commissioning editors; or from underground — on the literary black market. They look everywhere they can think of for themes — everywhere but inside their own heads, it doesn't enter their heads... to look there. Ah, if only they'd announce on that pillar in red letters three feet high: *Lecture in the Hall of Columns. On the Non-existence of Literature.* Oh, I'd show them..."

The speaker's voice rose to a dominant. Two or three passers-by glanced in our direction and slowed their step. The cumbrous listener shifted his knees and sat up. His face (the streetlamps were now spattering bright electric bile) wore an expression of disgust, or perhaps confusion. Oblivious, the theme catcher gripped his listener's shoulder and elbow with the fingers of both hands, as though he were a theme in need of molding. The theme tried to jerk his arm away and grumble something into his collar, but the theme catcher's voice, skipping from a high falsetto to a low apologetic whisper, restrained the recalcitrant elbow.

"You say this is 'nonsense'. Not at all: we writers write our stories, but literary historians in whose power it is to admit us or not to admit us into history, to open or slam the door, also want, you see, *to tell stories about stories*. Otherwise, they're stuck. And so the story that can be retold in ten words or less, the one easily summarized, squeezes in the door, while writings, which cannot produce that *something*, remain... nothing. Now, my friend, why don't you try..."

"I'm in a hurry."

"That's just what I need. Try, hurriedly, in a word or two, to annotate the meaning, to exgistolate the gist, if you will, of any popular modern work about this and that, or neither this nor that: as you please. Well, go ahead. Your choice and in a nutshell. I'm waiting. Aha, so you can't? Well then, put yourself in the future historian's place: he, poor soul, won't be able to either."

Having lost interest in his listener, the theme catcher turned abruptly to his right. At that end of the bench, a finger stuck inside his half-read book, an ear attentively cocked, sat a second silent witness to the discussion. He had long since given up reading so as to listen. The lower half of his face was muffled in a scarf, the upper half obscured by the long shadow of a visor.

Now the varicolored book cover resting on his knees caught the theme catcher's restless eye.

"Aha. I see you're reading that translation of Woodworth's *Bunk*. Amusing. Isn't it?"

The visor nodded its shadow in the affirmative.

"You see," the sharp-featured man burst out. "It hooked you. How? You haven't read it?" he glanced back over his shoulder. "No? Well then. The idea: to debunk all the bunk of which life is made. The plot: a writer, at work on a novel, discovers a character missing. The character has slipped out from under his pen. Work comes to a halt. One day, the writer happens to look in on a literary reading and is stunned to find himself face to face with his character. The character tries to run out the door. But the writer — I think this is how it goes — grabs him by the shoulder and elbow — like this — and says: 'Listen, just between us, you're not a person, you're a...' They end by agreeing not to spoil things for each other anymore and to devote themselves wholeheartedly to their common cause: the novel. The author introduces his character to an individual essential to the plot's development. This individual then introduces the character to a charming woman with whom he falls head over heels in love. The remaining chapters of this novel within a novel quickly begin to go awry and askew, like lines typed on a sheet that has popped out from under the bar. The author, upon receiving no new material from his love-besotted character, insists he break with the woman. The character tries to dodge, to play for time. At his wits' end, the author demands (this over the telephone) immediate submission to his pen or else... But the character simply hangs up. The End."

For some ten seconds the theme catcher regarded us all with a mischievous, almost childlike smile. Then a wrinkle appeared across his brow and his beard snagged on his fingers.

"No, that's not the end. The denouement is wrong. Misses the mark. I would... Hmm... let me just think. Now I've got it: they don't talk on the telephone, they meet face to face. The author demands — the character refuses. Before you know it, one has challenged the other. They duel. The character kills the author. That's it, can't be otherwise. When the woman, whom the pseudo-man has been vainly trying to win, discovers that she was the cause of the duel, she goes to him herself. But now the man-character cannot love, cannot not love, he can't do anything: without the author he is nothing, nil. *Punctum**. An ending like that would — I think — give a better approximation. Although..."

The speaker stopped short, shut himself up inside himself and suddenly, without looking at anyone, got to his feet and walked off. What happened next was even less expected: his listener, who had seemed to be waiting for the chance to get rid of this fanciful inventor, jerked up, as though attached by a string, and trudged resignedly after him.

The middle of the bench was now empty. The man at the end was absorbed in skimming the last pages of his book, evidently checking what he had just heard. Then he glanced over at me. We might have spoken. But just then a woman appeared and established herself between us. She powdered her nose then asked for a cigarette. Both I, and the man with the scarf-muffled mouth, remembered that the hour

---

* Period (*Lat.*)

was approaching when to speak of literature on Tverskoi Boulevard was not the custom. We nodded to each other, and went our separate ways: I to the left, he to the right.


3

My second encounter with the theme catcher came about just as unexpectedly. Two steps from where I live, elbow to elbow. Lost in thought, he looked up abstractedly at the purposeful touch of my hand.

"You must be mistaken or..."

"No. I stopped you in order to propose myself as a character. Or don't you take ones like me? In that case, I beg your pardon."

Smiling sheepishly, he regarded me, only half remembering. I reminded him: the bench on the boulevard — the novel's double ending — the series of themes. He nodded with sudden delight and, taking my hand, shook it warmly. I've noticed this before: people who live outside of things, surrounded by formulas and phantasms, are averse to the usual gradualnesses, they befriend one and reject one immediately and completely.

"What interests me," I said, turning serious as, like old acquaintances, we set off side by side I can't remember where, or rather, set off nowhere, "is your accusation of themelessness. Who or what is on the defendants' bench: a day in the life of contemporary literature or..."

He smiled.

"Sitting on that bench, which, as I recall, was just an ordinary boulevard bench, were you and I: I talked — you listened. And it all came down to a statement of fact, not an accusation. Moreover, 'a day in the life of contemporary literature', as you call it, is not or almost not to blame."

"But then I don't understand..."

"Not to blame," my companion insisted, "because... Incidentally, this reminds me of a caricature I once saw in an old English magazine: a girl and a stagecoach. In the first picture, the girl (she's carrying a basket) has caught up with the receding stagecoach; but to climb up onto the high footboard, she must put her basket down; having scrambled up onto the step, the girl turns round to collect her basket, but the stagecoach has already driven off; in the second picture, the poor girl jumps down, dashes back for her basket then runs after the lumbering stagecoach. She again reaches the step and this time settles her basket on it first; but while she is doing this, the stagecoach picks up speed, and the girl — in the third, and last, picture — exhausted and out of breath, plumps down in the middle of the road and bursts into bitter tears. By this I mean: the literary stagecoach will not wait, which is why the poet with poetry in hand, given conditions today, cannot possibly gain the elusive step: if the poet jumps into literature — then poetry is left behind, left out of literature; if poetry manages to attain the step, to attain an artistic level — then the poet, excluded and rejected, is left completely *out*. You, of course, disagree."

"I can hardly do otherwise. Still, my point in stopping you was not to refute your argument, but to ask you a question. Tell me, what do you think of the time when the stagecoach hadn't yet been hitched to horses? In other words, of poetry in the past, before the Revolution?"

He shrugged:

"I never think backward, only forward. But if for some reason you need me to... Though I'll probably say something absurd and beside the point."

"Please go on."

"You see, once upon a time, before the lifequake, so to speak, I made the acquaintance of a provincial counselor-at-law: crumpled collar, wife, children, greasy tailcoat — but attached to the top of his tattered briefcase with little metal screws was a chain of silver-plated letters: *Fire the hearts of men with the Word*. There. Now if that isn't clear, I'll try..."

"It's clear."

"Of course," my companion went on more quickly, "of course, the counselor-at-law disappeared long ago, together with all his effects, but the briefcase with its silver-plated 'Fire the hearts' survived. At least, I seem to have come across it once or twice. Though I can't say for certain: both times piles of papers and files were lying on top of it, but something in the expression of the tattered corners struck me... Right away I thought: that's it."

"What a strange man you are," I couldn't help smiling. "But please go on. Where did those mysterious meetings with the old briefcase take place?"

"The last one, if you'll believe it, was just the other day. In the office of a distinguished editor. Next to a red pencil and notepad. Why are you laughing?"

But in a second he too was chuckling, contorting his mouth like a child and twitching his eyebrows. Morose passers-by gave us a wide berth. I looked about: a half-familiar crossroads; intent stone rumors of a church tower; faded grass sticking up between the cobbles; and off to one side, behind low ranks of houses, muffled by a mute: the dull vibration of the city's strings.

We hadn't planned this. The conversation itself had led us to these silent and lonely purlieus.

I was the first to return to words:

"So you've been in those offices with red pencils. And your themes too?"

"Yes."

"What was the result?"

"Rejs."

"Meaning?"

"Well... The corners of my manuscripts were all marked: No. and Rej. I have a whole collection of *Rej*."

"You make it sound as if you'd collected them on purpose..."

"At first, of course, I didn't. But then I very nearly did. I no longer wondered whether my manuscript would be rejected, I only wondered *how*. Those people now in possession of the poor provincial solicitor's briefcase — with their manner of speaking, setting and resetting terms, arguing, penciling notes in the margins, pompously philosophizing, bowing and scraping before the telephone while eyeing their visitor with scorn, adjusting their pince-nez through which they see, *without* changing lenses, now close up, now far away, in accordance with the importance or insignificance of said visitor — these people gradually became, for me, a *theme*. Thereafter, my purpose in meeting with them was purely practical. For until I have fully elucidated a theme, until I have determined its source and uncovered every detail, I cannot rest. Ever. Yes, editors will have to go on dealing with my manuscripts and also with my eyes: until I hide them beneath my lashes.

"I ought to tell you that when I first arrived in Moscow (this was six years ago), I knocked right into the gigantic and unforgiving back of the Revolution. Walls minus many of their bricks were scrawled with shellbursts and drooling poster paints... Entrances were boarded-up. On my way to my first editorial office, on an outlying boulevard, I passed such an expressive bench (I shall never forget it): its back collapsed as if in a faint, and one spasmodic leg sticking obscenely up in the air. I had a collection of stories to propose. The title? Very simple: *Stories for the Crossed-Out*."

"What did the editor say?"

"'Won't do,' he said, and pushed it away having read only the title. In another place my bundle disappeared into the incoming mail and returned via the outgoing. In a third... but this is dull. On one manuscript I remember finding the penciled comment: *Psychologizing*. Only once did I encounter anything like scrutiny. Having leafed through my manuscript, the man behind the editor's desk inspected me with his sharp graphite pupils and, tapping his pencil, said: 'And you? Are you one of the crossed-out or one of the crossers-out?' I have to admit I hadn't expected a question like that. 'I don't know,' I said stupidly. The man pushed the manuscript towards me: 'Well, you ought to find out, and without delay, don't you think?' Blushing profusely, I rose to leave, but the editor stopped me with a gesture: 'Just a minute. You have talent. But you must put it into a pen, and the pen into your hand. Your stories are, well, how shall I put it... untimely. Put them away — let them wait. In the meantime, a person able to cross things out would, most likely, suit us. Have you ever tried writing criticism? A reappraisal, say, of reappraisals? You know what I mean. Do try. I'll look forward to reading.'

"I walked out feeling troubled and confused. There was something muddling about the man I'd left behind, behind that door. I remember I tossed all night, my elbows bumping against the hard theme that layers our entire life. My pen, as soon as I dipped it in ink, wrote: *Animal Disputans**. That was the title. Next came... perhaps this doesn't interest you?"

"Please go on."

"I took the title and the first verses of my song, if you will, from an old and long-forgotten book by the Danish humorist Holberg. This book — *Nicolai Klimmi Her subterraneum*, I believe it's called — describes the fantastic adventures of a traveler who winds up, I can't remember how, inside the Earth. The traveler is astonished to find that inside the planet, as inside a hermetically sealed vessel, lives a race with its own hermetically sealed State system, way of life, culture, everything that is customary in such cases. Over time the

---

* Arguing Animal (*Lat.*).

life of these undergroundlings — once rife with wars and
conflict, cut off, hidden away beneath miles of crust — sorted
itself out and settled into a harmonious routine. The problems
of the hermetically sealed were all solved, everything ironed
out and agreed upon. But in memory of those long-ago wars,
Nicolai Klimmi tells us — no, please listen, it's rather touching
— the land's noblest and richest magnates raised *animal
disputans*'es. There isn't anything to argue about in an isolated
country where everything has been determined and pre-
determined *in saecula seaculorum*\*, but these disputants
were trained for the purpose, fed a special diet that irritated
the liver and sublingual nerve, then pitted against each other
and forced to argue till they were hoarse and foaming at the
mouth — to unanimous laughter and merry halloos from the
lovers of old traditions... I did not draw any clear parallels.
But that squinty man behind the editor's desk understood
right away, from the first lines."

"I'm sure he did. And I suppose you never saw him
again."

"No. On the contrary. He even praised my writing: he
called it 'forceful' and 'sharp-edged'. But then, softly tapping
his pencil, he began to blame himself: as a seasoned editor,
he should have guessed... 'You,' he went on slyly tapping,
'are no prosecutor. Why not try writing for the defense, so
to speak, instead? Take some idea, social formula or class
type, and defend it? I can't promise anything, but...' 'You
think,' I burst out, 'that I would defend just anything?' 'Not at

---

\* For evermore (*Lat.*).

all,' he replied, sliding 'Animal Disputans' slowly back across the desk towards me: 'The choice of subject is entirely up to you. Needless to say. Good day.' What could I do? I left — and returned a week later with a new manuscript: 'In Defense of Rosinante.'"

"What a strange title."

"Well now he, my editor with the squint, didn't think so. The idea couldn't have been simpler. History, I wrote, had divided people into two classes: those who are on top (in the saddle) and those who are underneath (under the saddle): the Don Quixotes and the Rosinantes. The Don Quixotes sally forth on their fantastically marvelous and distant quests, straight to the idea, the ideal and the *Zukunftstaat*\*; all eyes, beginning with Cervantes' own, are on them and on them alone. No one cares about the winded and mercilessly lashed Rosinante: steel stars of spurs slash his bloodied flanks while his ribs dance beneath the squeeze of knees and cinch. It's time, high time this jade, bearing history on its back, heard something besides goadings. Gradually unfurling my theme, I then switched to..."

"What did your editor do?" I interrupted.

"Well, what else could he do? He gave me back my manuscript and said: 'I won't be seeing you again soon. Or ever, I'm afraid.' As I stepped towards the door, I heard him rise from his chair. I turned round: he was standing with his palm outstretched. We gave each other a warm handshake and, do you know, I felt that this man — even across the abyss between us — was close... closer than some of my

---

\* State of the future (*Ger.*)

close friends. Of course, we'll never meet again. And I imagine he's seen many more like me since."

For a minute the story stopped. Wasteland and kitchen gardens stretched all about us. Along a distant embankment, shavings of white locomotive smoke curled up into the air in elongated rings.

"There is a custom," he began again. "A very naive one. To help the soul, when it is passing through its trials, one places a saucer of clear water in the window: so that the soul may cleanse itself and endure further. But I was not given to see either the window or the saucer again. Over the next two years I asked nothing more of the briefcases. Yet I didn't give up writing. I was like one of those wild bees described by Fabre: even if you poke holes in their honey-combs, they will go on making honey; the honey drools through the holes, yet they, the sillies, go on making more.

"My situation was becoming direr every day. Dried fish and raw onions are cheap, I can tell you, but hardly nourishing. My pursuit of those elusive kopecks eventually led me inside a building where the many doors were numbered, the stairs steep as life. One of the literary bosses to whom I had applied for work turned out to be amiable and obliging. 'Sensitive topics,' he said, 'had best be put off; for the time being; as for great men, you may help yourself.' With that he pulled a sheet of paper out of a folder: a column of names — almost all of them crossed out ('for the crossed-out' flashed through my mind). The boss scratched his nose in annoyance: 'Those fellows grabbed the whole lot. But just a moment, just a moment, here's one that got away. Perhaps you'll have him:

Bacon. He's yours. Ten thousand words. For a mass audience. Now I'll just...' The boss was about to take his pencil to Bacon, but I stopped him: 'Which one shall I write about?' 'What do you mean — which one?' the good man looked amazed. 'There's only one Bacon — write about him.' 'There are two.' 'You must be mistaken.' 'I'm not mistaken: Roger and Francis.' The editor's face darkened, but only for a minute. 'All right,' he gave up. 'So there are two. Write: "The Brothers Bacon." Fifteen thousand words.' 'But just a moment,' I persisted. 'How can they be brothers when one is 300 years older?' The boss's face was no longer kind; he leapt to his feet and spat: 'You're all of you alike! I want to help, but you... Well, guess what! You can't have one, can't have two, can't have either!' Crossing the great empiricist out in his fury, he clapped the folder shut — and disappeared through one of the doors. I could only disappear through the other.

"I won't bore you with the whole forty days. One more of my trials will suffice. Friends, you see, had written a letter commending me to a top newspaper editor. I imagined that in that swift current I might set myself afloat more easily. The newspaper to which this editor belonged was, of course, red, though he himself had, in my opinion, his yellow spots. He agreed to a series of articles on pithy — or 'burning', as he put it — topics. 'Be good to have a unifying title,' he said. I thought a minute, and suggested: 'At Home'. He liked it. Advance in hand, I set immediately to work. My first article — on what I considered a burning topic — was called: 'Thirteen Ways to Recant'. Intended as a short guide, this piece listed all the ways to recant, from an open letter in a newspaper to... But when his eyes slid down to that *to*, my editor shook his head in grave reproach. His tone of exceeding solicitude turned to one of exceeding mistrust. I couldn't return the advance, so I had to settle my debt in words. In the end my signature appeared under a column of brevier, of which only the first third was mine, the rest was some sort of... I stormed into the editor's office brandishing the article. He heard me out, then snapped: 'You don't know journalism. I do. The only way we can work together is if you bring us facts and material (you have an eye, I won't deny it) and let us draw any conclusions ourselves.' I was too indignant to speak. He understood. We nodded to each other and parted ways... Why look, here's the cemetery."

Indeed, the string of reminiscences had led us to a vast and silent settlement of the dead, its crosses scattered about hills.

"Are you tired?"

"A little."

We entered the enclosure through a gate. The path wound first to the right, then in zigzags among the stooped and decrepit crosses.

"We could sit for a moment."

"Let's do. Right here."

We sank down onto the prickly greensward. The theme catcher stretched out his long legs and cast an eye over the tops of the crosses:

"Um-hmm. If you've come into this busy world, live your life and leave."

I looked at him in silence. Weariness had made his chiseled features even sharper. As if to turn a tight screw tighter, he added:

"I'd like a sleeping-car berth. For all eternity. And on the very lowest bunk. But that's nonsense."

His left hand began its mechanical dance up and down his coat-breast.

"I've been led here, to the dead, any number of times before. By my thoughts. I always think on my feet, on the move: sometimes I walk and walk, and there aren't enough streets, so then I wander in here, to this place of silence. The old watchman in the watch-box — do you see it? — over there by the gates, on the right? — is an acquaintance of mine. He once told me a very curious story. He couldn't have made it up. He heard a noise, you see. This was before dawn. He listened: a crowbar striking stone. A call to the police, a squad arrives — and together they steal between the graves towards the sound. In one of the vaults they see a light. They creep up. Stick their heads in the door, and see — hunched over an open coffin, a dark lantern in one hand — a back and moving elbows. They fall on the grave robber, drag him out — and what do you know! He's clutching a forceps, and in the forceps, trailing an extravagant root, is a gold tooth. He's a dentist (of sorts). 'The whole way to the station,' the watchman finished, 'the tooth-drawer cursed. Cursed and cursed. "Why take a working man from his work? Wore myself out with that corpse, and now I'll go to prison for my pains."'

"Well, I couldn't resist: I tried turning the incident into a story. I must still have it somewhere at home. It's about a burglar, no longer young, but respectable (in his circle, of course). I've forgotten his name — it was a good name, but I've forgotten it. Well, anyway — call him Fedos Shpyn. Shpyn's work is clean, conscientious, unerring. But he is increasingly hindered by that greatest of afflictions for a thief: deafness. A man past his prime can't easily change professions. Shpyn continues to do what he has always done. His hands never fail him, but his hearing... One day he's caught red-handed: prison. He has time to consider the theme: 'Life is no joke.' Then he's released. Without means. He tries to find 'an honest job'. At his age, he doesn't need much. But thousands of young men are also out of work; who needs a deaf one with no skills? Shpyn goes back to his old trade. And back to prison. He's a recidivist. They take him to the dactyloscopy room and press his fingers to a board coated with wax. When they toss the old man back into life, he feels that something has been pulled out of the ends of his fingers, stolen, and that without that something, numbered and stashed away in the files, it's even harder. The ancient burglar doesn't like (and never has) people with sharp ears. He shuns even his fellows: he thinks they're laughing at him behind his back, making fun of that deaf duffer Fedos Shpyn. No longer able to rob the living, he must practice among the dead. 'They,' Shypn muses, a smile spreading across his face, 'are even harder of hearing than I am.' But corpses, too, are a problem. Once upon a time people dressed the dead in their best, their cold fingers in rings and precious stones, their stiff feet in polished boots. But now the appurtenances were grown shabby and mean, the aim being — it's a disgrace, really — to stick a person in his coffin (no one will see, they say) in just his socks and some moth-eaten garment. 'If this keeps up,' Shpyn reflects as he picks his way home at night through the puddles from some suburban cemetery, 'before a person's even cold they'll be (they'll figure it out, they will) yanking the gold out of his lifeless mouth themselves, and they'll do it slapdash, in a hurry, without technique. What do they care? But I'll be without a living.' One day Shpyn sets off to work: come to a crossroads, he cups his palm to his ear — are bells tolling anywhere? He can't tell; he hears only dulled rustlings and rumblings. He lingers by a sign that says: Coffins. Sometimes you can pick up a scent here. No one. He trudges to the nearest church porch: standing on the steps is a woman in black — so he peeps inside: there it is, surrounded by burning candles, and the mourners are neatly and expensively dressed. 'A good sign,' thinks Shpyn, 'only how can you tell what he's got under his lips? Gold or cement? Or maybe nothing at all. He's not a horse — can't look in his mouth.' A priest and deacon come out of the altar gates, one candle lights another, muffled voices float down from the choir loft — Shpyn more divines than hears them — they promise eternal rest among the saints in a land without grief and lamentations. Reflecting that soon he too will be tucked under a blanket of turf, old Fedos sighs and crosses himself. But with the last prayer, the professional in him awakes: he joins the line, hands pressed decorously to his breast. The file of mourners brings Shpyn up to the coffin. He leans over and — peering into the crack between the blue, petrified lips (jolts have forced them slightly apart) — spies two golden glimmers. Having kissed the corpse, Shpyn steps aside: his face wears the quiet satisfaction and seriousness of a man ready to perform his sad duty to the end. Someone in the crowd looks respectfully at Shpyn then whispers to his neighbor: 'What beautiful sorrow!' The procession is moving. Shpyn's rheumatic legs barely obey, but he mustn't give up now. He shuffles after the casket amidst relatives and friends. A young man takes him deferentially by the elbow. Having mentally counted off all the bends in the paths (he'll have to work by night, after all) and memorized the place, the old man quits the cemetery. The rest of the day he dozes, warming his frozen feet by the stove. That night, he packs up his tools and again makes the final journey. And then... but the ending can be taken alive from the watchman's story. Life is stranger than fiction. Well, shall we go? It's getting late. They'll lock the gates."

We strolled out onto the main path, past the church and office. By the office window, my companion paused and peered inside.

"What are you doing?"

"Go on ahead. I'll catch you up."

And, indeed, by the time I had reached the gates he was at my side and smiling in response to my inquiring look.

"I wanted to see if it was still there. It is."

"What?"

"The wreath for hire. They have one here. The watchman told me so. A wreath for poor people. You pay twenty or thirty kopecks, you see, and a proper metal wreath with porcelain forget-me-nots and long black ribbons is brought out to meet the procession, to attend the last rites, and then repose on the grave, full of dignity and grief, lavish and inconsolable. But as soon as the mourners have gone, the watchman fetches it back to the office: to wait for the next casket. What I am about to say may strike you as funny or perhaps absurd, but I feel a brotherly affection for that wreath. For aren't we, the poets, like elegant wreaths erring from grave to grave? Don't we too, with all our meanings and with all our being, nestle beside the dead and buried? No, no. I shall never agree with the briefcases' current philosophy: one can write only about the crossed-out and only for the crossed-out."

We walked on, elbow to elbow, along the broad outlying streets. Soon we saw the smooth parallels of tram tracks coming toward us. And hard by my shoulder I heard the quiet remark:

"If parallels converge in infinity, then all trains that disappear into infinity must, at the convergence, meet with disaster."

We walked two or three blocks without exchanging another word. I was plunged in my thoughts when my companion's sudden voice made me start:

"If I haven't worn you out completely I'd like to tell you my last theme. I've often wanted to write it down, but I'm afraid I'll spoil it. It's not long. It won't take ten minutes; or perhaps I shouldn't?"

With a shy smile, he looked at me almost pleadingly.

"No, by all means."

And the story began.

"I want to call it 'The Funeral Repast'. Only this is not about cemeteries. No, no. It's subtler than that. A fellow with a wife, a three-room apartment, a servant, a good salary and a good name, is entertaining friends. The table is littered with empty dishes and bottles, a small glass of toothpicks. The guests repair to the study, to sit by the fire and discuss a recent film, a recent decree, where best to go for the summer. The fellow's wife produces a box of old photographs and family mementoes. The fellow rummages in the cardboard piles and suddenly, from the bottom of the box, comes the soft tap of glass. What could it be? He pulls out a phial: the transparent phial is stopped with a cork and inside is a tiny white crystal. Puzzled, the fellow removes the cork and, wetting a finger with saliva, presses it first to the crystal, then to his lips: he gives his guests a sly and mysterious smile. Understanding neither smile nor crystal, they question their host with a dozen eyes. But he demurs. His brow twitches, his eyes narrow. No longer smiling, he looks as though he were trying to remember a dream. His impatient guests crowd round him: 'What is it?' His wife tugs at his shoulder: 'Stop torturing us.' Then the man says: 'Saccharine.' His friends roar, but he is not laughing. When they have quieted, he says: 'I have an idea, let's organize a funeral banquet. In memory of the days when we were hungry and cold. What do you say?' — 'You always were a joker.' — 'What an eccentric...'

"Then again, why not? Books have become boring, the new plays have all been seen, and winter evenings are long and uneventful. They settle on a day and separate amid hoots of: 'No other group of friends would...' — 'Are the trams still running?' — 'What an eccentric...'

"On the appointed day, the master of ceremonies wakes his wife at dawn: 'Get up — we have to get ready.' She has forgotten all about it, and besides: 'Why rush about at this ungodly hour? The guests aren't coming till this evening.' But her eccentric joker insists. He wakes the servant and sets to work: 'Glasha, open the casement windows and let the cold air in; raise the dampers and don't fire the stoves. Take the wood out of that box — that's right — and stuff the rug in there. Why? In case there's a requisition. Won't fit? Then roll it up — that's right — there you go... Move all the things from the bedroom and dining room into my study. Won't fit? Of course they will — and so will we. We'll all be living in the study because we can't heat three rooms. You? You won't be here — I can't afford a servant.' Stunned and frightened, Glasha thinks she must still be asleep and dreaming some absurd dream. But the joker reassures her: 'Just for today. Tomorrow everything will be as it was, understand?' Glasha goes on gawping. But when the master says she may have the day off once she's finished with the furniture, her face brightens, and bureaus, divans and tables bang, clatter and scrape their way into the study. Now fully awake, the master's wife tries to put her foot down: 'What can you be thinking of?' — 'Not I, we. Now help me to take this shelf down from the wall.' The whole day the house is bustling: must go to the apothecary for saccharine, can't buy rotten flour anywhere, forgot to add bran to the bread and mix in bits of straw — nearly in tears, the eccentric's wife kneads the stiff and dirty dough a second time. The study is crammed and clogged with a fantastic conglomeration of things, and still the stubborn man goes up into the attic to hunt for the small iron stove: that rusty absurdity, jabbing its iron trunk into whatever it can, occupies the last free lozenge of floor space.

"When the man, grimy with smuts and covered in rust, gets up off his knees, he sees his wife wrapped in a wool shawl, huddled in a corner of the divan with her knees tucked under her chin. She is watching him with angry and frightened eyes. 'Marra, do you know,' he touches her shoulder (the shoulder jerks away), 'Marra, that's how you looked seven years ago, like a frozen sparrow, in a shawl and fur coat, miserable and forsaken, and I — do you remember? — I drew your icy fingers out from under your shawl — like this — and breathed on them — like this, like this — until you said: "That's better."' His wife says nothing. 'Or do you remember how I brought you that comical ration in six tiny paper cones (a mouse couldn't have eaten its fill), and we did all our cooking on this old pile of rust — more smoke and soot than food.' — 'But the kerosene stove was worse,' his wife replies, still facing away, 'this one at least warmed us, but that one... and the flame was dim, "sickly", as you said.' — 'And here you won't even look at it.' — 'And when only a few matches were left in the box,' his wife goes on, oblivious, 'I'd cut them up lengthwise — so that one match made four.' — 'Yes, and I couldn't do that, my hands were so clumsy.' — 'No, you've forgotten, your fingers were simply frostbitten, that's all.' — 'No, no, Marra, my darling, my hands are clumsier.' The man feels a soft shoulder touch his, hears the tender voice that makes his temples sing: 'Oh, how wonderful they were, those long evenings together, just the two of us: if we stirred at all — so did the flame in the oil lamp — and the shadows from things would flicker, up-down, up-down, over the table, the walls, the floor. So silly and merry. Did you get the oil lamp?' — 'No.' — 'Why not? We can't do without that.' — 'It went right out of my head,' the man jumps up. 'Never mind, I'll make one. Meanwhile, you unscrew the light bulbs; like this — see how easy it is, you don't even need a ladder, just climb up onto the tables.'

"The guests begin arriving. Each one first rings the bell and listens for footsteps, then knocks, and finally bangs on the door. 'Who is it?' — asks their host through the chain on the lock. Some don't understand, others get angry, but still others respond in kind. 'Have to knock louder,' their host explains, 'can't hear you through two rooms.' He leads them — one by one — through the dark and empty room cubes to the last, inhabited one. 'Better keep your coats on, we're working on the stove, but it's still around freezing.' The guests shift uneasily from foot to foot, not knowing where to put themselves or what to do. One thinks with dismay of the opera ticket he gave away so as to hang about — who knows why — beside an idiotic oil lamp, in this bleakness and cold; another regrets not having dressed more warmly. Their host seats them on odd trunks, stands, and stools, and suggests they warm themselves with tea. 'Carrot tea,' he says proudly, pouring the boiling swill into mugs of various sizes. 'Very hard to come by. And here's the saccharine. Help yourselves. But be careful — or the tea will be sickeningly sweet.' Slices of bread cut into identical squarelets are divided up even Stephen. The guests bring the smoking mugs reluctantly to their lips. Someone notices that steam is coming out of his mouth. Silence.

"The host tries to start the conversation going. 'What do you think,' he turns to his neighbor, 'when will the warm weather arrive?' — 'In two or three months,' says his neighbor, burying his nose in the carrot steam. 'My dear sir,' the man who traded the opera for a funeral bursts out, 'how can you be so cavalier? Throwing months around like that. It seems funny now, but in those years — it's true — we calculated to the day. You'd form a sort of working hypothesis that the spring would arrive the 1st of March — all at once and for good. Then every morning you'd count the days: fifty-three days till spring, fifty-two till fine weather, fifty-one till that long-awaited day. And here you say: two or three months. At the winter solstice, we would gather in a small group and clink cups of this same carrot mash, drunk at the mere thought that the sun had turned in its orbit and was now coming towards us. And you say: two or three months.'

"The conversation, as if it has been stirred in a glass with a spoon, whirls along, faster and faster, gathering everyone up in its course. Empty mugs reach for the kettle. In the heat of an argument, someone swallows his bread-square whole and tries to cough up the bit of straw stuck in his throat.

"'No, listen. Do you remember,' cries the man who forgot to dress warmly, 'do you remember how during that hard December frost we'd pull on our hats (our coats were always on, after all, even inside), and scramble over the snowdrifts — the only source of light besides the stars — to go and hear that lecturer... what was his name, I've forgotten, he later died of typhoid. He would pace, poor soul, from wall to wall, like a caged wolf — and talk about the cosmos, the Revolution, the new problems, crises in life, in art. And when he paused, his mouth would dive under his muffler for a sip of warmth. The air was bitter cold and flecked with flickering shadows (as it is here). We sat there for hours, shoulder to shoulder, and a thousand eyes followed him — from wall to wall, from wall to wall. Our feet grew numb, our soles stuck to the icy floor, but not a rustle, not a murmur. Hush.' — 'I went to those readings too,' the host recalls musingly. 'One day he told us that before the Revolution, we did not see the world because of things, we were lost in our possessions; we would only gain, he said, by giving everything away — from the intelligible to the indoor (let them load them onto carts, down to the bare walls, give the walls away too, and the roof over your head) — all things in exchange for the supreme thing: the world.'

"The guests begin to leave. They all shake their host's hand with warm gratitude. On his way out through the empty echoing rooms, the man who gave his ticket away admits to his companion: 'I gave lectures then, too — to political instructors.' — 'About what?' — 'About ancient Greek vases.'

"The hosts are alone again. The iron stove has gone out

and is growing cold. The draught from a door has doused the flame in the oil lamp. The two sit shoulder to shoulder, in the darkness. The city flashes and rattles on the window-panes. But they don't hear. 'Breathe on my fingers... the way you did then.' — 'Will you say: "That's better"?' — 'Yes.' He caresses her small palms — first with his breath, then with his lips. Words are so easy to hide inside those meek and tender palms. And the man says, 'Beyond that door is an empty room, and beyond it another empty and dark room; and further still are more dark and empty rooms; and beyond them; and you'll walk and walk, and not...' Marra suddenly feels prickly warm drops on her fingers, mixing with his breath and words.

"And here — at the end — I want to show that even these harmless lovebirds, these anonymous people on the sidelines, whom the Revolution only grazed — even they, even they cannot help but understand..."

Something suddenly clanked and blazed three steps ahead of us, blocking our path, and came to a stop with a clang: a tram. A second later another bell, shuddering wheels and — before our eyes in the empty air — through the gloaming — under three red lights: *Flag Stop*. The theme catcher caught my inquiring look and shook his head:

"No, that's not it. And perhaps there is no 'it' to be invented for this theme. I'm crossing it out: the devil take it!"

I even turned round to look: I had the absurd, but distinct sense that the theme was there, behind us, on the rails, cut in two by the wheels.

The city was rushing towards us. Automobiles were

droning and rumbling, spokes were spinning, horseshoes were clopping, and along the street — up, down and all around — people were walking. My companion gave me an anxious look: his eyes and even his bristly beard had an apologetic and ingratiating expression (as though asking forgiveness for the sadness he had inadvertently caused). Almost begging me to smile, he remarked:

"I have a friend, a former philosopher, and whenever we meet he says: 'What a life! Don't even have time to contemplate the world.'"

I somehow couldn't smile. We turned into the boulevard where it was quieter and less crowded. The theme catcher trailed behind me wearing a rather caught expression himself. He clearly would have liked to rest on a bench. But I strode resolutely on and did not look back. We passed the bench that had introduced us. Suddenly, at the end of the boulevard: a tight motionless ring of people shoulder-to-shoulder, necks craning towards the center of the circle. We too walked up: music. The sharp squeak of a bow, up-down, and thin whistling sounds struggling to make a melody. I glanced round the circle, then at my companion; he was leaning wearily against a tree, and also listening; his face was intent and proud, his mouth, like that of a daydreaming child, slightly open.

"Let's go."

We tossed our kopecks into the case, crossed the square, and tramped down Nikitsky Boulevard. At the crooked prospect of the Arbat, we stopped; I was searching for my final parting words.

"I hesitate to call it 'gratitude', but believe me..." I began, but he — as usual — interrupted:

"And even the Arbat. I always associate it with the Arabat Spit. That sandbar is as curved and as narrow, only it continues for a good sixty miles. You know — you could make a story out of it: summer; southbound trains chockfull ('Where are you headed?' — 'What about you?'); and one passenger who does not answer and does not ask; no baskets, no suitcases — just a light knapsack and a staff; he changes to a branch line — Alekseyevka — Genichesk; very few people at first — an almost empty caterpillar of cars, then a tiny Godforsaken town. But the passenger dons his sack and, having thrown a coin to the boatman who has ferried him across the sound to the end of the spit, begins his sixty-mile walk. People would call this walk strange, but there are no people here: the blade of the Arabat is utterly deserted, legs and staff encounter only sand and shingle, rotten seas are either side, a sun-scorched sky above, and ahead an endless strip, narrow and dead, leading on and on. In effect, in the whole world there is only that... but you're in a hurry, and I'm gabbling. I've already stolen... a day not mine."

I took his hand, and for a long time we held each other's gaze. He understood:

"So there's no hope?"

"None."

I hadn't gone more than a dozen paces when — through the noise and hubbub of the square — his voice overtook me:

"And even so!"

I turned round.

He was standing on the curb, smiling brightly and serenely, and repeating, no longer to me, but to the starburst of streets before him:

"And even so."

Those were our final parting words.

4

As soon as I got home I stretched out on the daybed. But my thoughts went on pacing inside my head. It wasn't until almost midnight that the black bookmark of sleep lay down between that day and the next.

Only in the morning, as I let in the sun waiting behind the curtains, did I remember my non-metaphorical bookmark tucked away in the desk drawer. I must, without further delay, attend to its fate.

I first fetched a notebook, then half opened the drawer: the bookmark was still lying on the yellow bottom, having primly smoothed out its faded silk train, an ironic expectant expression stitched into its design. I smiled at my bookmark and again closed the drawer: this time in earnest.

Three workdays went into recording all of this: with mirror-like exactitude I described our two meetings, banishing all words not his, and ruthlessly crossing out all those fellow travellers who would insinuate themselves into the story and be woven into the truth.

When the notebook was ready, I again opened the door of my solitary blue-silk bookmark's prison: and we again began our wanderings from line to line inside the notebook.

The bookmark often had to wait for me, as it had in those long-ago years, now at one theme, now at another; we mused and dreamed, we squabbled *no against no*, making our dilatory and fitful way — from step to step, from paragraph to paragraph, following the theme catcher's images, meanings, expositions and endings; I remember we spent nearly half of one night over that short, nine-letter: "*And even so...*"

Of course, my old bookmark's quarters are — for the moment — cramped and squalid. But that can't be helped. We all live flattened, we all live in pinched quadratures, cooped up and resentful. But any corner is better than the long, bare literary pavement of today. Well then, I think that's all. Oh yes, I nearly forgot: on the cover of the notebook I must write — as is customary — the name of the tenant: BOOK MARK.

*1927*

# Yellow Coal

1

The economic barometer at Harvard University had continually pointed to bad weather. But even its exact readings could not have predicted such a swift deepening of the crisis. Wars and the elements had turned the earth into a waster of its energies. Oil wells were running dry. The energy-producing effect of black, white and brown coal was diminishing yearly. An unprecedented drought had swaddled the sere earth in what felt like a dozen equators. Crops burned to their roots. Forests caught fire in the infernal heat. The selvas of South America and the jungles of India blazed with smoky flames. Agrarian countries were ravaged first. True, forests reduced to ashes had given place to ashy boles of factory smoke. But their days too were numbered. Fuellessness was threatening machines with motionlessness. Even glacier snowcaps, melted by the perennial summer, could not provide an adequate supply of waterpower; the beds of shrinking rivers lay exposed, and soon the turbine-generators would stop.

The earth had a fever. Flogged mercilessly by the sun's yellow whips, it whirled round like a dervish dancing his last furious dance.

If nations had ignored political strictures and come to each other's aid, salvation might have been theirs. But adversity only exacerbated ideas of jingoism, and soon all the New and Old World Reichs, Staats, Republics and Lands — like the fish on the desiccated bottoms of erstwhile lakes — were covered with a viscous sheath, swathed in borders like the filaments of cocoons, and raising customs duties to astronomical levels.

The one agency of an international sort was the Commission for the Access of New and Original Energies: CANOE. To the person who discovered a new energy source, a motive power as yet unknown on earth, CANOE promised a seven-figure sum.

2

Professor Leker was too busy to notice people. Blinkered by diagrams, thoughts, and pages from books, his eyes had no time to reflect faces. A frosted screen before the window shielded him from the street; the black case of an automobile, window curtains drawn, did likewise. Until a few years ago Leker had taught, then gradually given it up to devote himself full-time to his research into quantum theory, ionization, and the vicariate of the senses.

Thus Professor Leker's twenty-minute stroll, his first in ten years, was pure accident. Leker set out in the company of his thoughts, without noticing places or faces. But the very first crossroad threw him into a quandary. The scientist was obliged to lift his head and gaze about to get his bearings. And here, for the first time, the street grated against his pupils.

A dingily bilious sun suffused the air through a tent of black clouds. Spitefully elbowing elbows, passers-by rushed along the pavement. People converged in the doorways of shops, tried to pummel their way through and stuck fast, faces flushed with rage and exertion, teeth bared.

The steps floating along the tram tracks were jammed with passengers: chests tried to climb up on backs; but the backs, flicking spiteful shoulder blades, would not budge; hands all in a tangle gripped the vertical handrails with rapacious vigor — like flocks of carrion crows fighting over prey.

The tram passed by, and behind it, as behind a curtain drawn back, a new scene unfolded across the street: two fist-shaking men were verbally assaulting each other; a circle of gloating pupils instantly formed round them and circling the circle another circle and another; while above the melee of shoulders raised sticks hovered.

Looking about him, Leker walked on. Suddenly his knee knocked into an outstretched hand. Protruding from dirty rags, the hand was demanding a donation. Leker dug in his pockets: he had no money on him. The open palm continued to wait. Leker again searched himself: nothing except a notepad. Without taking his gaze off the beggar, he stepped aside: the cripple's eyes, half blind with pus, oozed with slime and an insatiable, impotent spite.

With greater and greater misgivings, Professor Leker scrutinized the street, gnashing with steel rims and humming with anxious human swarms. The people changed, yet remained the same: jaws clenched, foreheads butting the air, elbows endlessly elbowing their way. The famous physiologist first raised his eyebrows in astonishment, then knit them together the better to contain the thought fluttering behind them. Leker slowed his step and opened his notepad, searching for the exact words. Suddenly the stab of someone's elbow deep in his ribs sent him staggering sideways: he hit his back against a post and dropped his slips of paper. Yet even the pain could not stop Leker smiling: his thought, tightly tied with associative threads, had been flung to the bottom of his brain.

### 3

The competition announced by CANOE drew nearly a hundred entries, each with its own motto. Among these was that of Professor Leker. Most of the entries consisted of theoretical or practical impossibilities; a few others, subjected to a more serious discussion, afforded some semblance of a solution but required too great a capital investment. The competitor who devised the motto Oderint* might well have lost to the witty and subtle scientific proposal to force the Sun itself to pay for the damages it had inflicted on the planet: increased solar activity in certain parts of the world should, this project said, be stimulated to temperature levels capable of accomplishing work by converting heat into mechanical energy. The idea of putting the sun in harness to rebuild the globe's half-ruined industry was close to winning the seven-figure prize, but... the corners of the commission chairman's

---

* Come to hate (*Lat.*).

eyes had a yellowish tinge, while the lenses of the deputy chairman's pince-nez betrayed a prickly glint.

Both men favored the Sun-harnessing project, but the chairman, who was loath to agree with the deputy chairman, switched his vote at the last minute to spite him — and *Oderint* tipped the scales.

To its next closed meeting, the commission invited Professor Leker. Asked to state his idea in brief, Leker began:

"My project is simple: I propose to use the energy of spite inhabiting countless individuals. On the long keyboard of feelings, you see, the black keys of spite have their own distinct, sharply differentiated tone. Whereas other emotions — tenderness, let's say, or affection — are accompanied by a loss of muscle tone, a certain relaxation of the organism's motor system, spite is entirely muscular, it's all in the tensing of muscles, the clenching of fists, the gritting of teeth. But this feeling has no outlet: it is muted, muffled, and socially dimmed, like a lamp, which is why it produces soot, but no light. Yet if one were to remove the mufflers, if one were to allow all that bile to burst the social dams, then this yellow coal, as I call it, would set our factories' flywheels spinning again, a million lamps would shine with electric bile and... I must ask you not to interrupt... How can this be done? If I may have a piece of chalk I will draw you a diagram of my myeloabsorberator: AE perpendicular at 0; here, at an angle, the panel's entire surface is stippled with absorbent apertures.

"You see, the idea of exteriorizing muscular effort (which I've guided through all the interstices of my brain) is entirely feasible. For if we take the junction of nerve and muscle, then we see that the nerve fiber carrying the energy charge, strives, by splitting into very fine fibrils, to encase the muscle in a sort of — the sponge, if you please — net. Krause gave us the first histological description of this, but the credit for this exact picture of the nerve net's weave belongs to me. Hmm... Now what was I just... Oh, yes. The problem is this: to catch the net in a net, and bring that catch to shore, outside, beyond the confines of a person's skin. Now if you will look at the absorberator's stipple of apertures, you will see that..."

Leker spoke for nearly two hours. His last word was followed by several minutes of silence. Then the chairman, the yellow corners of his eyes gleaming, said:

"That's all very well, but are you sure that those reserves of human spite, which you propose to exploit, are sufficiently large and dependable? For here one would be dealing not with a stratified deposit, awaiting a pickaxe, but with an emotion that ebbs and flows. Do I make myself clear?"

Professor Leker replied with a dry:

"Perfectly."

The commissioners were tight-lipped as to the possibility of using yellow coal for industrial purposes. They decided that the project had best begin on a small scale and confine itself to prospect mining.

4

Here is what happened early one morning before office hours on the outskirts of a European capital. A two-car tram trundled round the loop and up to the tram stop, teeming with harried briefcases. Briefcases poured into both cars, oblivious in their haste to the somewhat unorthodox construction of the car behind: a yellow stripe ran down its shiny red side; thin thread-like wires sprouting from the handrails plunged under the car's metal skin; the brass seats were stippled with microscopic apertures that disappeared somewhere deep inside.

A bell tinkled from car to car, the driver ducked down between the buffers, then ran back to his seat; he flicked the main switch; and the car in front, now quit of its crowded trailer, sailed away. The bewilderment of the passengers in the abandoned car lasted but a few seconds. Hands thrown up in surprise began, one after another, to clench into fists. Spite, inflamed by its own impotence, set all mouths in motion.

"What is this, leaving us in the middle of the street, like rubbish?!"

"Scoundrels!"

"Have you ever seen such a thing? Filthy wretches!!"

"Ought to be locked up..."

"I'd strangle them with my bare hands first..."

Just then, as if in answer to the splatters of spit and venom, the trailer, with a soft screech of axles, started up. It had no trolley on top, the driver's seat was empty, and yet, mysteriously gaining speed, the car whirred along in pursuit of its mate. Passengers exchanged anxious glances; a woman let out a desperate scream: "Help!" Panic ensued, and the car's entire contents lunged for the doors. But no one would let anyone past. Shoulders pressed against shoulders, elbows against elbows; this firm human dough kneaded itself with a hundred wedged fists. "Out of my way!" "Move over!" "Let me through!" "I can't bre-e-eathe!" With that, the car, which had just begun to slow down, rocketed off at full speed. Tumbling off the steps onto the painful pavement, passengers gradually vacated the incomprehensible trailer. Then its wheels stuttered to a halt. Ten yards short of the next tram stop. Without listening to explanations, a new crowd of passengers scrabbled aboard, and a minute later, steel grinding against steel, the car's yellow stripe was again cleaving the air.

That evening the extraordinary trailer was shunted back to the park, but its photographic image continued to roam inside the pupils of millions of buyers of evening papers. The sensational news set all the wires humming and loudspeakers screaming. That date soon became known as the beginning of a new industrial era on earth.

5

During the first months of industry's gradual changeover to yellow-coal energy, it was feared that the reservoirs of spite deep inside humanity might soon be exhausted. Various projects, ancillary to Leker's own, proposed methods of stimulating spite artificially — in case natural supplies should fall off. Thus the famous ethnographer Krantz published his *Classification of Interethnic Hatreds*, a two-volume work asserting that humanity should be split into the smallest possible ethnicities so as to produce the maximum "kinetic spite" (Krantz's term). But the anonymous author of a pamphlet entitled "Once One Is One" went further: he advocated reviving the ancient adage *bellum omnium contra omnes*, the war of all against all. The war *contra omnes* of post-history would, he reasoned, differ radically from that of pre-history. If the "pre" set all men against each other because of their lack of an "I", of humanity, the "post" would create a conflict between excesses of "I": once put into practice, every "I" would lay claim to the whole earth and all its riches. This eminently logical philosophical system would saddle the earth with some three billion absolute monarchs and, therefore, countless wars of aggression and spite, the approximate number of which could be determined by calculating all possible combinations of one individual against three billion other individuals and multiplying that number again by three billion.

Most popular of all, however, was a book by psychologist Jules Chardon, *The Optical Couple*. A master of the art of metaphor, Chardon began by comparing twin stars to married couples. As in astronomy, which says that twin stars may be either physical, i.e. a function of one star's proximity in space to another, or optical, when stars separated by dozens of light years are brought into proximity by the angle of the eye of the beholder, so in matrimoniology, which studies the combinations of two people most profitable to mankind. If until now love, that system of matrimonial reflexes, profited the State, then with the switch to the use of spite-driven bodies, the institution of marriage would have to be reformed: the rate of optical marriages would have to be increased gradually to 100%. Coldness and, wherever possible, repugnance multiplied by proximity would produce high-voltage spite, which need only be sucked into individual pocket absorberators and transmitted along wires to a central accumulator that would distill all spite, the entire flow of bile, into a common yellow reserve.

It would be difficult to list all the methods proposed for increasing supplies of absorberator-grade spite. In any event, it soon became clear that these artificial stimulators were all but unnecessary — the natural reserves of this energy in its various forms, ranging from disgust to fury, were indeterminably vast and, evidently, inexhaustible.

It turned out that the energy of a potential fistfight, if sucked promptly into the pores of a street absorberator, was enough to heat an entire floor of a building for twelve hours. Even without taking any matrimoniological measures, if one simply furnished two million "happily married" couples with so-called porous double beds, one could fuel the work of an enormous sawmill.

Life was changing and being reequipped at a feverish pace. The doorways of offices and shops were narrowed to make it easier for their invisible pores to collect the energy of bodies shoving in and shoving out. The turnstiles on boulevards, the backs of theater seats, worktables and workbenches were all fitted with special porous devices to absorb emulsions of bile, turning drops into streams, streams into floods, and floods into boiling bubbling seas.

Surges of hatred, fits of anger, paroxysms of rage plunged into wires and reemerged as the steel squeals of saws, the vibrations of pistons and the grinding of gearwheels.

The day's ill will waited in an accumulator to be allowed,

once yellowed into the coals of arched streetlamps, to low softly over the ray-spangled night.

### 6

Mister Francis Deddle was against the bilification of life, and he was not alone. No need to look very far: his parish priest and his wife's sister, a girl of about forty with the hands of a very devout scullery maid, felt the same way. Sermons from several pulpits had already denounced the yellow delusion polluting the world. A papal encyclical — delayed for some reason — was expected shortly.

The opposition was gradually rallying its forces, and while supporters of the total conversion of industry and culture to yellow coal sneered that the anti-bilists were nothing but soutanes and skirts, in fact they underestimated their adversary's numbers. The sheet the protesters put out — *Heart Versus Liver* — was quite popular.

Mr. Deddle was a founding member of the Heartist Organization and one of its most active. True, he had to work with his hands tied. The government viewed heartist propaganda as wrecking the yellow construction. Philanthropic societies were forced to close, and sermons to be heard by empty pews. As a result, the Heartist Organization was up against the wall (and those walls were stippled with absorberizing apertures)...

One morning Mr. Deddle woke up feeling extremely depressed. Under his door, along with the latest issue of *Heart Versus Liver*, was an envelope. He opened it: a directive from the Heartists' Central Committee:

"Sir, Within two hours of receiving this letter, you must love humanity. A good example is the beginning of salvation."

Mr. Deddle fiddled with the piece of paper and knew that the day was ruined. The hour hand on the clock showed nine. Catching sight of the Roman numeral eleven, Mr. Deddle muttered, "Well, we still have time" and, squinting, tried to picture that hazy many-headedness called humanity. Then he raised himself up on his elbow, opened the newssheet and glanced over the headlines: "Oh no! Well, well... So that's it! Damn!" He crumpled the paper up and threw it on the floor: "Now be calm, be calm, old man, come eleven o'clock you'll have to..." Deddle smiled musingly and began to dress. On his way past the crumpled newssheet, he bent down, picked it up and carefully smoothed out the wrinkles.

At a quarter to ten Mr. Deddle sat down to breakfast. Two or three slices of ham to start, followed by the tap of his teaspoon on the top of a boiled egg. The yolk, welling up out of the shell like an evil eye, reminded him that... Mr. Deddle suddenly lost his appetite and pushed the plate away. The hour hand was edging towards ten. "I really ought to, hmm, do something. I can't just sit here." But just then the telephone's metallic ring shuddered through the air. "I won't answer it, they can go to the devil!" The telephone paused then began ringing again with greater urgency. Deddle pressed his ear to the instrument with a feeling of annoyance:

"Hello! Yes, speaking. Call back after eleven. I'm busy right now: with a matter of importance to all mankind.

Urgent? So is this. What? I'm busy I tell you, and you keep insisting, like a..."

The receiver returned incensed to its hook. Mister Deddle, hands clasped behind his back, began pacing from wall to wall. His eye happened to light on the thin, graduated glass tube protruding from the absorberator, which had covered his wall, as it had walls in all the rooms in all the world, with its barely visible pores. The mercury in the glass indicator, clinging to the numbers, was slowly rising. "Can I really be...? No, no. I must get to work!" Deddle went to the window and peered out at the life in the street: the pavement was, as always, black with people; they were thronging the sidewalks, pouring out of all the doors and gates.

"Sweet humanity, dear humanity," Deddle stammered. He could feel his fingers tightening involuntarily into a fist, and prickles shivering — vertebra by vertebra — down his spine.

The windowpanes rattled and knocked with the hoarse hoots of motor-car horns, while the crowd's soft flesh, squeezing out of every crack, went on being kneaded by the walls of the street.

"Dear people, my brothers, oh, how I..." Deddle's teeth grit. "Good Lord, how can it be? Twenty to eleven, and I..."

Deddle curtained the street and, trying not to look at the indicator, sank into an armchair.

"Let's try *in abstracto*. Exert yourself, old man, and love those worthless scamps. If only for a quarter of an hour, if only a little bit. Go on and love them just to spite them. Damn, it's already five to. Oh Lord, help me! Work a miracle, let all men love their neighbors. Well, humanity, get ready, because here I go: my beloveds..."

A soft glassy tinkle made Deddle start and turn his face, beaded with sweat, towards the absorberator: the indicator tube, unable to withstand the tension, had exploded, spraying mercury all over the floor.

7

Though plagued by failure at the outset, the technique of extracting and accumulating yellow coal eventually improved to the point of ruling out accidents such as the one just described. The very word "failure" ceased to mean what it had: for it was life's failures, the embittered malcontents, who adapted best to the new culture. Their grudge against life had become remunerative, the source of a nice income. The entire human race underwent retraining. Portable counters, worn by one and all, determined one's rate of payment based on the amount of spite one radiated. The slogan BE ANGRY OR GO HUNGRY floated in huge letters above every crossroad. The good-natured and softhearted were thrown out onto the street where they either died or became hardened. In the latter case, the numbers on their individual counters surged and kept them from starving to death.

Even before Leker's idea was put into practice, a special CANOE subcommittee had been formed to study the possibility of exploiting class hatred. The subcommittee worked in secret: CANOE members well understood that this kind of hatred required extreme caution. The conversion to yellow coal had naturally caused unrest among workers in obsolete industries. Meanwhile, the capitalists, closing ranks around CANOE, had resolutely rejected the old policy of attempting to appease workers with grievances against the exploiter class. Now that hatred of exploitation could be... exploited for industrial purposes, collected by an absorberator and pumped into engines and machines. Mills could make do with workers' hatred alone; the workers themselves were no longer needed. Factories and mills began laying huge numbers of people off, keeping only skeleton crews to man the spite-collectors. The wave of protests and strikes that swept the globe only increased the bilious energy in accumulators and gave good dividends. It turned out that the very purest spite — it hardly needed to be filtered — came from the unemployed. At the first conference on spite collection, a venerable German economist declared that a bright new era was dawning when work could be done with the help of strikes. A guarded swash of gloating applause greeted his words. Indicator needles on absorberators in the conference hall trembled slightly.

8

Indeed, the world had entered a kind of Golden Age. And no need to hack through the earth's crust for the gold, no need to rinse it in streams — it seeped out of the liver on its own in yellow granules which rinsed themselves in the circulation of the blood, it was right here, under layers of skin. One's liver had become a tightly stuffed and miraculously inexhaustible purse that one carried not in one's pocket, but deep inside one's body where no thief could get at it. It was convenient and portable. A tiff with one's wife bought a three-course meal. The hunchback's envy of his well-proportioned rival allowed the hunchback — once he had shifted the gold in his, so to speak, inside pocket to an outer one — to console himself with a high-priced cocotte. All in all, life was getting cheaper and easier by the day. The energy from accumulators was building new buildings, expanding cramped quadratures, turning shacks into palaces, dressing existence not in gray sackcloth, but in elaborate and colorful costumes; the precipitate flood of bile, transmuted into energy, washed the soot from the sky and the filth from the earth. If before people had been jammed together, knocking into each other, in small dark cubbyholes, now they lived in vast, high-ceilinged rooms whose wide-set windows stood open to the sun. If before cheap boots, as though stung by their cheapness, had bit into one's heels with their nails, now neatly sewn soles floated like velvet underfoot. If before the village poor had shivered by unheated stoves, their hunger-hollowed faces concealing a hopeless, centuries-old spite, now that reservoir of spite gently warmed the snakelike coils of their radiators, creating coziness and ease. Now everyone was well fed. Instead of yellow bristles, plump rosy cheeks. Figures gained inches; stomachs and gestures became round, and livers coated with a soft fatty film. That was the beginning of the end.

Outwardly everything seemed fine: machines working at full tilt, the human flood pressing against the cracks of doorways, yellow-coal accumulators transmitting energy along wires and through the air. But now and then, here and there, something unforeseen and at first seemingly insignificant began to happen. Thus on a fine late summer day in Berlin, for instance, police detained three people who would not stop smiling. This was outrageous. The chief of police, his florid face half choked by his tight yellow collar, stamped and screamed at the delinquents:

"Today you take it into your heads to smile in a public place, tomorrow you'll be running through the streets naked!"

The three smiles were convicted of hooliganism and made to pay a fine.

Another incident was far more serious: a young man on a tram had the temerity to give up his seat to an old crone, half-flattened by the press of elbows and shoulders. When the impudent fellow was shown § 4 of the Rules and Regulations for Passengers — *Giving up one's seat is punishable by a prison term of up to...* — he refused to take his seat back. As for the old crone, she too, according to newspaper reports, was shocked by the lout's behavior.

A rash of puzzling incidents began to spread over the globe's gigantic body. Highly symptomatic was the scandalous trial of a schoolteacher who had announced during a lesson:

"Children should love their parents."

His pupils, of course, did not understand the archaic word "love" and asked their parents what it meant; many parents, too, could not recall. But *their* parents made plain the odious phrase, and the corrupter of youth was sent before a jury of judges. But in a still more sensational twist, the judges acquitted the villain. Now the government began to fret. The yellow press (the press of that period was all yellow) raised a hue and cry, demanding that the ruling be overturned. Pictures of newly appointed judges ran in all the special editions: yet their faces, plastered across those sheets, were strangely amiable, plump and insouciant. As a result, the corrupter remained at large.

Emergency measures had to be taken. Especially since not only yellow opinion, but yellow industry was beginning to break down. The teeth of the mechanical saws at one factory, as if tired of chewing wood fibers, suddenly stopped. The wheels of trains and trams were turning a little more slowly. The light inside glass lampshades was slightly tarnished. True, the accumulators, still filled with centuries of rage, could feed power-operated belts and pinions for four or five years to come. But supplies of their new, living energy were dwindling by the day.

The governments of all nations were making every effort to avert a crisis. They needed to artificially raise spite radiation to its former level. They decided to cut off people's heat and electricity periodically. But those people with their bankrupt livers simply sat, patiently and uncomplainingly, in their enormous dark rooms and didn't even try to move closer to their cooling stoves. Had it been possible, it would have been pointless to turn on a light to see the expressions on their faces: their faces wore no expression at all. They were vacant, rosy-cheeked and mentally dead.

Now doctors were brought in. They prescribed pills to

activate the liver, also liquids and electric stimulation. All in vain. The liver, having said all it had to say, had wrapped itself in its fatty cocoon and fallen fast asleep. No matter how they bombarded it with patent medicines, increased doses, and radical therapies of all sorts, the result was of no value to industry.

Time was running out. Everyone knew it: the sea of bile was ebbing, never to flow again. New sources of energy would have to be found thanks to a new Leker, whose discovery would reorganize life from top to bottom. CANOE, phased out in recent years, went back to work. The commission appealed to inventors around the world for help. In response they received almost nothing of any significance. Inventors there were, but their inventiveness had vanished along with their spite. Now nowhere could one find — not for a seven-, eight- or even nine-figure sum — the old embittered minds, the furious inspirations, the pens sharp as stingers and dipped in bile. Today's insipid ink, devoid of blood and bile, pure and unfermented, produced nothing but silly scribbles and vague, blot-like thoughts. The culture was dying — in disgrace and in silence. In its final years, amidst the expanding entropy of amiability, not even one satirist could be found to make proper fun of the rise and fall of the age of yellow coal.

*1939*

# Notes

INTRODUCTION (pp. 6-11)

*Georgy Shengeli*: (1894-1956), a well-known poet in the 1920s and '30s, a literary critic and translator of classics (Byron, Heine, Hugo, Verlaine, Baudelaire).

*Severyanin*: Igor Severyanin (1887-1941) was a popular Silver Age poet and a founder of Ego-futurism. The poem alluded to is *Na zakate* (1927).

*Leskov*: Nikolai Leskov (1831-1895). Best known for "Lady Macbeth of Mtsensk", this highly original writer was underrated in both Tsarist and Soviet times.

*Adalbert von Chamisso*: (1781-1838), was born at the Château de Boncourt in Champagne. His family fled France during the Revolution and settled in Berlin where Chamisso became a linguist, a naturalist, a poet and a writer. In 1815 he was appointed botanist to the Russian ship *Rurik* on a scientific voyage round the world. He published a diary of that three-year expedition but is mainly remembered for his ballads and for *Peter Schlemihl* (1814).

*Mikhail Bulgakov*: (1891-1940). The Kiev-born novelist and playwright had arrived in Moscow six months before Krzhizhanovsky. The diary entry quoted is from 9 February 1922.

*Maksim Gorky*: (1868-1936), then the greatest and most powerful authority on literature in the Soviet Union.

*Socialist Realism*: the basic method of Soviet literature, first imposed in 1932 when Stalin famously declared writers to be "engineers of human souls".

QUADRATURIN (pp. 14-28)

*Re-measuring Commission*: Created by the Soviet authorities in the early 1920s, this commission re-measured rooms in order to determine who had "excess" living space. One person was entitled to no more than 9 sq. meters (97 sq. feet). In this respect, Sutulin had nothing to fear.

IN THE PUPIL (pp. 29-69)

*Quagga*: a South African mammal (*Equus quagga*) related to the ass and to the zebra, but striped only on the fore part of the body and the head; now extinct.

*Telegony*: the supposed influence of a previous sire upon the offspring subsequently borne by the same mother to other sires.

*Lord Morton*: "In Lord Morton's famous hybrid from a chestnut mare and male quagga, the hybrid, and even the pure offspring subsequently produced from the mare by a black Arabian sire, were much more plainly barred across the legs than is even the pure quagga." — Charles Darwin, *The Origin of Species* (1859).

*Mr. Ewart*: James Cossar Ewart (1851-1933), Scottish zoologist and professor of natural history. His pioneering experiments in animal breeding and hybridization disproved the theory of telegony.

*Ebbinghaus*: Hermann Ebbinghaus (1850-1909), German experimental psychologist who devised methods of measuring rote learning and memory.

*Thales*: (c. 624-546 B.C.), the Greek philosopher, scientist and mathematician, was the first thinker to try to explain natural phenomena by searching for causes within nature itself, rather than in mythology.

*Weber-Fechner Law*: This law, originated in 1834, states that the intensity of a sensation is proportional to the logarithm of the intensity of the stimulus causing it.

*Kant*: Immanuel Kant (1724-1804), the German philosopher and author of the *Critique of Pure Reason*, the *Critique of Practical Reason*, and the *Critique of Judgment*.

## AUTOBIOGRAPHY OF A CORPSE (pp. 81-120)

*The hum of a primus-stove*: In her book *The New Russia* (1928), the American journalist Dorothy Thompson recalls the "subdued roar" of the primus, "the one-burner oil stove, which more than any institution in modern Moscow asserts the eternity of the individualist."

*Had I not vacated my hundred sq. feet by hanging myself*: Krzhizhanovsky's own room in Moscow (see Introduction) had evidently been occupied by a dead man. Alexander Naryshkin, a regional vice-governor before the Revolution, was living at Arbat, 44, Apt. 5, when he was arrested in 1919. He died in prison in 1921.

*Stirner*: Max Stirner (1806-1856), German philosopher who embraced psychological and ethical egoism; the author of *The Ego and Its Own*.

*Gogotsky*: Silvester Gogotsky (1813-1889), philosopher born in Kiev; the author of Russia's first multi-volume dictionary of philosophy (*Philosophsky Leksikon*).

*Obviously a strike*: An apparent reference to one of several large student protests at Moscow University at the beginning of the 20th century.

*The Manège*: The military riding school built in 1817 opposite the Kremlin.

*Herberstein*: Sigismund von Herberstein (1486-1566), Austrian diplomat, historian, and author of *Rerum Moscoviticarum Commentarii* (or Notes on Muscovite Affairs). The book was written in Latin and based on his extended visits to Muscovy in 1517 and 1526.

*Rabelais*: Francois Rabelais (1494?-1553), French priest, physician and writer. Rabelais' dying words are said to have been: "*Je vais querir un Grand Peut-Etre*" (I go in quest of a Great Perhaps).

*The city in which I lived changed hands thirteen times*: The Ukraine had been part of the Russian empire until the monarchy collapsed in February 1917. During the anarchy that followed, Kiev changed hands no fewer than 12 times as the Russians, the Soviets, the Poles and various Ukrainian factions fought for supremacy.

THE UNBITTEN ELBOW (pp.121-135)

*The unbitten elbow*: This title derives from a Russian idiom (*blizok lokot, da ne ukusish*, literally "your elbow is near, but you can't bite it") used to denote something that seems easily doable or within reach but is in fact undoable or out of reach. "So near and yet so far" is the rough English equivalent.

*That age-old gnoseological drama*: Gnoseology is the philosophic theory of knowledge: inquiry into the basis, nature, validity and limits of knowledge.

*Stirnerianism*: see note on Stirner under "Autobiography of a Corpse".

*The verse in the Bible that says that "the length thereof" was sixty cubits*: (1 Kings 6:2): "And the house which king Solomon built for the Lord, the length thereof was threescore cubits..." The Russian word for "cubit" is the same as that for "elbow": *lokot.*

*Spencer's argument with the dead Kant*: Herbert Spencer (1820-1903), the English philosopher and sociologist, rejected Kant's claim that Space and Time are subjective conditions.

*Neo-Lamarckism*: a return to the ideas of Jean-Baptiste Lamarck (1744-1829), the French biologist who claimed that acquired traits could be inherited. (This notion would be discredited by most geneticists by 1940 — except in the USSR.)

THE BOOKMARK (pp. 136-183)

*Vita Nuova*: (c. 1293), a short work by Dante composed of 31 sonnets and connecting prose commentaries.

*They had equipped the inside of its pointed crown... with global vibrations and radio signals*: A permanent radio station was installed at the top of the Eiffel Tower in 1906.

*Lake Constance*: occupies an old glacier basin bordering Switzerland, Germany and Austria.

*A fashionable Boston religion*: a reference to Christian Science.

*One of Metner's Fairy Tales*: Nikolai Metner (1879-1951), the Russian composer, wrote many genre pieces for pianoforte, including a series called 34 Fairy Tales.

*February — July — October*: 1917. That is, from the February Revolution through the July Bolshevik putsch to the October coup.

*That translation of Woodworth's Bunk*: William E. Woodworth, a pedestrian American writer, was a harsh critic of the capitalist system. In the late 1920s, the Soviet Union published three of his now long-forgotten novels.

*Fire the hearts of men with the Word*: The last line of Pushkin's poem "The Prophet" (1826) about the role and purpose of the poet.

*Holberg*: Ludvig Holberg (1648-1754) is claimed by both Norway and Denmark as a founder of their literatures. His satirical *The Journey of Niels Klim to the World Underground* appeared in 1741, the Russian translation in 1762.

*Those wild bees described by Fabre*: Jean Henri Fabre (1823-1915), French entomologist. He demonstrated the importance of instinct in insects.

*"How can they be brothers when one is 300 years older?"*: Roger Bacon (c. 1214-1294), English philosopher, scientist and Franciscan; Francis Bacon (1561-1626), English philosopher, essayist and statesman.

*Genichesk*: town at the northern end of the Arabat Spit.

*Arabat Spit*: In the Crimea, a long and very narrow sandbar running north to south between the Sea of Azov and the Gniloe (the Russian word for "rotten" or "decayed") Sea.

YELLOW COAL (pp. 184-202)

*The vicariate of the senses*: The substitution of the senses, as in the sharpened remaining senses of a blind man.

*Krause*: Wilhelm Krause (1833-1910), German anatomist.